GRUESOME GHOULS
OF
GRAND RAPIDS

Here's what readers from around the country are saying about Johnathan Rand's *AMERICAN CHILLERS:*

"I just read Terrible Tractors of Texas, and it was great! I live in Texas, and that book totally freaked me out!"
-Sean P., age 9, Texas

"I love your books! Can you make more so I can read them?"
-Alexis B., age 8, Michigan

"Last week, two kids in the library got into a fight over one of your books. But I don't remember what book it was."
-Kylee R., age 9, Nebraska

"I read The Haunted Schoolhouse in three days, and I'm reading it again! What a great book."
-Craig F., age 12, Florida

"I got Invisible Iguanas of Illinois for my birthday, and it's awesome! Write another one about Illinois!"
-Nick L., age 11, Illinois

"My brother says you're afraid of the dark, which is silly. But my brother makes things up a lot. I love your books, though!"
-Hope S., age 9, California

"I love your books! Make a book and put my name in it. That would be sweet!"
-Mark P., age 10, Montana

"I'm writing to tell you that THE MICHIGAN MEGA-MONSTERS was the scariest book I've ever read!"

-Clare H., age 11, Michigan

"In class, we read FLORIDA FOG PHANTOMS. I had never read your books before, but now I'm going to read all of them!"

-Clark D., age 8, North Carolina

"Our school library has all of your books, but they're always checked out. I have to wait two weeks to get OGRES OF OHIO. Can't you do something about this?"

-Abigail W., age 12, Minnesota

"When we visited Chillermania!, me and my brother met you! Do you remember? Anyway, I bought DINOSAURS DESTROY DETROIT. It was great!"

-Carrie R., age 12, Ohio

"For school, we have to write to our favorite author. So I'm writing to you. If I get a letter back, my teacher says I can read it to the class. Can you send me a letter back? Not a long one, though. P.S. Everyone in my school loves your books!"

-Jim A., age 9, Arizona

"I LOVE AMERICAN CHILLERS!"

-Cassidy H., age 8, Missouri

"My mom is freaked out by the cover of POISONOUS PYTHONS PARALYZE PENNSYLVANIA. I told her if she really wanted to get freaked out, read the book! It's so scary I had to sleep with the light on!"

-Ally K., age 12, Tennessee

"Your books give me the chills! I really, really love them, but I don't know what one I like best."

-Jeff M., age 12, Utah

"I was read WISCONSIN WEREWOLVES, and now I'm freaked out, because I live in Wisconsin. I never knew we had werewolves."

-Angie T., age 9, Wisconsin

"I have every single AMERICAN CHILLER except VIRTUAL VAMPIRES OF VERMONT. I love all of them!"

-Cole H ., age 11, Michigan

"The lady at the bookstore told me I should read NEBRASKA NIGHTCRAWLERS, so I did. I just finished it, and it was GREAT!"

-Stephen S., age 8, Oklahoma

"SOUTH CAROLINA SEA CREATURES is the best book in the whole world!"

-Ashlee L, age 11, Georgia

"I read your books every night!"

-Aaron. W, age 10, New York

"I love your books! When I read AMERICAN CHILLERS, it's like I'm part of the story!"

-Leroy N., age 8, Rhode Island

"KREEPY KLOWNS OF KALAMAZOO is my favorite. It was awesome! I did a book report about it, and I got an 'A'!

-Samantha T., age 10, Illinois

Don't miss these exciting, action-packed books by Johnathan Rand:

Michigan Chillers:

#1: Mayhem on Mackinac Island
#2: Terror Stalks Traverse City
#3: Poltergeists of Petoskey
#4: Aliens Attack Alpena
#5: Gargoyles of Gaylord
#6: Strange Spirits of St. Ignace
#7: Kreepy Klowns of Kalamazoo
#8: Dinosaurs Destroy Detroit
#9: Sinister Spiders of Saginaw
#10: Mackinaw City Mummies
#11: Great Lakes Ghost Ship
#12: AuSable Alligators
#13: Gruesome Ghouls of Grand Rapids

Freddie Fernortner, Fearless First Grader:

#1: The Fantastic Flying Bicycle
#2: The Super-Scary Night Thingy
#3: A Haunting We Will Go
#4: Freddie's Dog Walking Service
#5: The Big Box Fort
#6: Mr. Chewy's Big Adventure
#7: The Magical Wading Pool

American Chillers:

#1: The Michigan Mega-Monsters
#2: Ogres of Ohio
#3: Florida Fog Phantoms
#4: New York Ninjas
#5: Terrible Tractors of Texas
#6: Invisible Iguanas of Illinois
#7: Wisconsin Werewolves
#8: Minnesota Mall Mannequins
#9: Iron Insects Invade Indiana
#10: Missouri Madhouse
#11: Poisonous Pythons Paralyze Pennsylvania
#12: Dangerous Dolls of Delaware
#13: Virtual Vampires of Vermont
#14: Creepy Condors of California
#15: Nebraska Nightcrawlers
#16: Alien Androids Assault Arizona
#17: South Carolina Sea Creatures
#18: Washington Wax Museum
#19: North Dakota Night Dragons

Adventure Club series:

#1: Ghost in the Graveyard
#2: Ghost in the Grand
#3: The Haunted Schoolhouse

www.americanchillers.com

Johnathan Rand's

MICHIGAN CHILLERS

#13:
Gruesome Ghouls
of
Grand
Rapids

Johnathan
Rand

An AudioCraft Publishing, Inc. book

Michigan Chillers #13: Gruesome Ghouls of Grand Rapids
ISBN 978-1-893699-86-1

Cover Illustration by Dwayne Harris
Cover layout and design by Sue Harring

Printed in the USA

First Printing - February 2007

GRUESOME
GHOULS
OF
GRAND
RAPIDS

1

I first found out about the wood elves when I was only four or five years old. I was playing in our backyard in Grand Rapids, Michigan, when I saw a very small girl sitting on a tree branch.

And when I say 'small', I mean *small*. The girl was only eight or nine inches tall! We started talking, and she told me she was a wood elf, and that she lived in the forest with many other elves. She looked sort of like a fairy: she was dark-complected, and had thin wings on her back. She uses them to glide through the air. Her hair is dark, like mine, only hers is a lot longer. And the clothing she wears is made from green leaves.

Now, I know this may be hard for *you* to believe, but remember: I was very young. It never occurred to me that wood elves weren't supposed to be real.

When I told my mom and dad about the wood elf, they just laughed. They thought it was cute that I had an 'imaginary' friend. I tried to tell them the wood elf was real, that I wasn't making it up. Still, Mom and Dad just smiled. My older brother, Rick, just laughed at me.

Well, that was a long time ago. I'm almost twelve now . . . and I've become good friends with a few wood elves. The girl—Lina is her name—comes to my house a couple times a week. She's really smart, and she helps me with my math homework. Two other wood elves, Deepo and Mirak, stop by once in a while, too. There are many more wood elves, they tell me, but they live in a tall tree in the forest not far from my house.

And another thing: I'm the only one who can see them, as far as I can tell. Which is probably the reason that Mom, Dad, and my brother thought the wood elves were my imaginary friends. They can't see them, and I don't think anyone else can see them, either. I asked Lina about it, and she said it was because I was special. I didn't know what she meant by that, but I thought it was cool.

So, I don't talk about the wood elves to anyone, because people will think I'm weird. When Lina comes to my house to visit, I make sure that I speak quietly, so my mom, dad, and brother won't hear. They might think I'm talking to myself. Once, I almost told my best friend, Darius Perry, about the wood elves. But at the last second I decided not to. I didn't think he would believe me.

One morning, before I left for school, Lina appeared at my window. I smiled, but my grin quickly faded when I saw the worried expression on her face.

I slid the window open, and chilly, April air washed inside. All the snow had melted the month before, but the mornings were still cold. It would be another few weeks before it got warm and the flowers started to bloom.

"Hi, Lina!" I said.

"Hello, Ashlynn," Lina replied.

"What's wrong?" I asked as she jumped from the windowsill to my dresser.

Just then, my bedroom door opened and Mom poked her head in. Lina never moved from the dresser, because she knew I was the only person who could see her.

"Ten minutes, Ashlynn," Mom said.

"I'll be ready," I replied. I ride the bus to school every day, and my brother and I have to be at our bus stop at eight o'clock sharp, or we'll miss it.

Mom left, and I turned to Lina.

"Be careful today," she warned.

"Be careful of what?" I asked.

Lina looked around my room, and her wings fluttered a couple of times.

"Just . . . just be on the lookout for anything strange," she said.

"Like what?" I prodded.

Lina really looked nervous. I'd never seen her this way before.

"Creatures," she whispered.

"Creatures?" I echoed. "What kind of creatures?"

"It's a long story," Lina said. "I don't have time to tell you now. But you're able to see us, so you might be able to see the creatures, too."

"What kind of creatures are you talking about, Lina?" I asked.

"Ghouls," Lina said with a shudder and a flutter of her wings.

"Ghouls?" I said, getting a little nervous myself.

"I'll tell you more when you come home from school," Lina replied. "Until then, just be careful. You might be able to see the ghouls. If you can, they'll know it. They can't move very fast, though, so you should be able to outrun them if you have to."

This was all very confusing.

"What do they look like?" I asked.

Lina shook her head, and her dark hair fell over her shoulders. "Later," she replied. "After you get home from school."

Her wings flitted, and Lina darted to the windowsill and peered outside. Then, she looked at me.

"Just remember what I told you," she said. "I'll explain everything tonight." Then, she leapt from the window, glided through the air, and landed on the branch of the blue spruce tree that grows near my room. Lina vanished within the thick, needle-covered branches.

I went to school. Throughout the day, I wondered what Lina had meant.

Ghouls? I thought. *What did she mean by that? She's never talked about ghouls before.*

And I kept my eye out, but I didn't see anything out of the ordinary . . . until I got home.

That's when I discovered something waiting for me, hidden in the shadows of the trees that grew near our garage . . . .

2

That afternoon, the bus dropped me off at the end of our block. Usually, my brother rides the bus with me, but he had basketball practice.

I was alone.

I started to walk home. A cold wind chilled my face, and I shivered beneath my windbreaker. The sky was gray and dreary, and it looked like it might rain at any moment. Trees, their limbs empty of leaves, looked liked bundles of gnarled wires. I couldn't wait for warmer weather to arrive.

I walked along the sidewalk, gazing at the homes that lined the street. We live in a nice neighborhood. Some of the houses are big, and some, like ours, are smaller. Our home is on a dead-end street surrounded by trees. Behind our house, the forest is very thick, and there are lots of trails that wind through it. In the summer, I go for walks in the woods with my friends. Right now, however, the trails were still muddy from the long, cold winter.

A car went by, and a horn honked. I turned to see Mrs. Walker, our neighbor who lives across the street. Mrs. Walker is really nice. She has a big, black dog named Max. Max is very friendly. Once in a while, Mrs. Walker lets me take him for walks. She keeps him in her house, but she has a big fenced-in backyard where the dog runs around and plays. Sometimes, however, he jumps the fence and gets out . . . but he always comes back. I wish we could have a dog, but Dad says no.

I waved to Mrs. Walker, and she waved back. We have a lot of really nice people on our block.

My backpack was getting heavy, and I shifted it to my other shoulder. I had two pages of math homework, and I hoped that Lina would help me with it.

But I was more interested in what she'd promised to tell me about the ghouls. She hadn't told me what they look like, what they do, or anything. She had just warned me to be on the lookout for them.

Oh, well, I thought, as I turned to walk up our driveway. *I'm sure Lina will tell me tonight.*

And that's when I saw it.

A movement. Out of the corner of my eye, I saw something move by the side of our garage where the thick row of cedar shrubs grow. Cedars are like pine trees: they don't lose their leaves or needles in the winter.

And the ones growing next to our garage were tall . . . almost as tall as my dad. When my brother and I used to play hide-and-seek, I would hide in the branches all the time.

But what if there was something *else* hiding there right now?

What if it was one of those things that Lina warned me about?

A ghoul?

I stopped walking and stood in the driveway, looking at the cedar shrubs next to the garage.

Nothing moved.

I peered into the thick, spiny foliage, but I couldn't see anything but branches.

And then—

A branch moved!

I didn't know what to do. Should I run inside our house, or should I race into the forest to find Lina?

All too late, I realized I wasn't going to have time to do either. More branches moved and rustled, and a dark shape began to emerge.

Oh my gosh! I thought. *It's what Lina warned me about!*

A ghoul!

I opened my mouth and drew in a breath, preparing to let out the loudest scream I could muster. I didn't know what the ghouls were capable of doing, but Lina had seemed very worried about them. I was sure the creature was probably awful-looking . . . and dangerous.

Then, the ghoul shouted.

"Ouch!" he exclaimed as the branches parted.

I heaved a huge sigh of relief. It wasn't a ghoul! It was Darius Perry!

"What are you doing in there?!?!" I shouted, walking toward him.

Darius looked up and saw me approaching. "My softball," he replied. "I lost it yesterday, when we were playing. I thought it might be in the bushes."

"You scared me," I said. "I . . . I thought you were a—"

I stopped speaking. After all, I couldn't tell Darius that I thought he was a ghoul! He would think I was crazy!

"You thought I was a *what?*" Darius asked.

"Oh, nothing," I replied. "You just surprised me, that's all," I said. "Did you find your softball?"

Darius shook his head. "No," he said with a shrug. "I've looked everywhere. I think it's gone for good. Besides," he continued, "I have a ton of math homework. I'd better get started on it."

"I have a lot of math homework, too," I said. "It'll probably take me all night."

"It'll take me longer," Darius said. "You're a lot better at math than I am."

I smiled. I couldn't tell Darius that Lina helped me with my homework. Oh, she didn't give me the answers or anything. That would be cheating. But she showed me how to solve the problems on my own. As a result, I was getting a good grade in math . . . even though I didn't particularly like the subject.

"I'll see you later," Darius said. "If you happen to find my softball, bring it to school tomorrow, will you?"

"Sure," I said. "See you later."

Darius trudged over the lawn and across the street.

I felt silly, being scared like I had been. But, then again, Lina had warned me to be careful and to be on the lookout for ghouls. I was anxious for her to tell me more about them. I wondered what they looked like.

I walked toward our house . . . but a noise in our garage made me stop.

Turning to look, I didn't see anything out of the ordinary. Mom's red car was parked in its normal spot, and there was an empty space where Dad normally parks his white car. He was still at work.

I peered into the garage for a moment, but I didn't see or hear anything. It was probably just the wind.

But when I turned away, I heard a scratching sound.

Like claws. Claws on cement.

I spun . . . just in time to see the shape of a big, dark creature lunging for me!

I dropped my backpack and turned to run . . . when I heard a yelp.

Not just any yelp, either . . . but a *happy* yelp. A *dog's* yelp. A yelp that I'd know anywhere.

I turned around to see Max, Mrs. Walker's dog, bounding toward me. His mouth was open, and his tail was wagging like crazy.

A wave of relief rolled over me, and I dropped to my knees as Max approached.

"Hey, buddy!" I said, scratching the dog behind his ears. "You scared me!" I patted his head, and Max instantly rolled onto his back and raised his paws in the air, indicating he wanted his tummy rubbed.

"You silly thing," I said, scratching his belly. Max closed his eyes, enjoying the attention. "Come on. Let's get you home."

I stood, and Max followed. Then, I picked up my backpack and carried it to the porch.

"Mom!" I hollered, after I'd opened the door. "I'm going to take Max over to Mrs. Walker's house."

"Don't be long," she said.

"I won't," I said. "I'll be right back."

I dropped my backpack on the floor and closed the door.

"Come on, Max," I said. "Let's get you home."

I began walking across the yard, and Max followed. I wondered how the dog had escaped. Usually, he jumped the fence. Once in a while, he would dig a hole under it. That made Mrs. Walker mad, because it ruined the lawn.

I stopped at the curb to make sure there were no cars coming. Then, I continued across the street. Max sniffed at the pavement like a bloodhound.

When we reached the sidewalk on the other side of the street, Max suddenly stopped. His ears stood straight up, and he had a puzzled look on his face.

"What's up, you silly dog?" I asked.

Max gave me a quick glance and wagged his tail, then continued looking around curiously.

So, I looked around the neighborhood. At the end of the block, a car was backing out of a driveway. Other than that, there wasn't much going on.

"Come on," I said, and started walking. I crossed the street to Mrs. Walker's house. Her car was in the driveway, so I knew she was home.

And whatever Max had heard or spotted, he must have forgotten about it.

I skirted the side of Mrs. Walker's garage, intending to let Max into the backyard through the gate. Then, I would go to the front door and tell Mrs. Walker that I'd returned her dog.

But when I reached the fence and looked into the yard, I stopped and stared. What I saw was awful . . . and I knew, right then, that something was very, very wrong . . . .

5

In Mrs. Walker's backyard, a large hole had been ripped through the chain link fence! I knew right away that Max couldn't have done it, because the fence was made of metal. There was no way Max—or any dog, for that matter—could have done it. The fence was shredded, like it had been ripped apart by some sort of—

Monster.

That's what I *thought,* anyway. The fence had been peeled back and savagely torn apart, exposing frayed, jagged points. Something very strong had ripped a large hole in the fence.

Max was standing obediently by my side, waiting for me to open the gate.

"No," I said to the dog. "Let's go around front. I can't put you in the backyard, because you'll just get out again."

I walked, followed by Max, to the front of the house, where I rang the doorbell. Mrs. Walker came to the door a moment later.

"Well, if it isn't Ashlynn Meyer," she said with a smile. But when she saw Max on the porch, her smile faded. "Max," she scolded gently, pointing to the dog and wagging her finger. "Did you get out of the backyard again?"

"What happened to your fence, Mrs. Walker?" I asked.

Mrs. Walker looked puzzled. "What's wrong with it?" she asked. It was clear she was unaware her fence was damaged.

"There's a big hole ripped in it," I replied. "I think that's how Max got out this time. Go look. I'll meet you back there."

Mrs. Walker opened the door, and Max bounded inside the house. I turned and leapt off the porch, sprinting over the lawn and driveway, rounding the side of the garage, heading to the backyard. I stopped at the gate, lifted the latch, and pulled it open. Then, I closed it behind me and walked to where the fence had been damaged.

Mrs. Walker was already there. Her hands were on her hips, and she looked shocked.

"How in the world did this happen?" she asked. "Max couldn't possibly have done it. The fence looks like it's been torn apart by a bear."

Which was unlikely. We have bears in Michigan, but not where we live. And I couldn't think of any other animal big enough or strong enough to rip apart a metal fence.

"Well, I suppose I'd better call the police to report the damage," Mrs. Walker said. "Until it gets fixed, I'm going to have to keep an eye on Max, so he doesn't run off again. Thank you for bringing him back."

"No problem," I replied with a shrug. "I'd better get home, though."

I said good-bye to Mrs. Walker and let myself out through the gate. Before I walked away, I turned around and took one last look at the torn fence.

Lina's soft voice echoed in my head.

Ghouls, she had said. *You might be able to see the ghouls. If you can, they'll know it.*

I have to admit, I was a little scared.

Did a ghoul rip a hole in the fence? I wondered. *What do they look like? How big are they? Are they vicious?*

I turned to head home . . . and received the answer to all my questions.

Standing in the driveway, looking right at me, was the most horrible, hideous beast I had ever seen in my life! He was huge . . . and when he realized I'd spotted him, he attacked!

6

For a moment, I couldn't move. My skin knotted, and it felt like it was sliding off me. That's how scared I was! The ghoul was *huge!* I was sure he was at least a foot taller than my dad . . . maybe even bigger. His head was big, too, and it seemed abnormally large compared to his body. His mouth was open in a snarl, and I could see both his upper and lower teeth, which looked like they were in desperate need of a good brushing.

Then, he started coming toward me. His movements were jerky, and he seemed to be a little clumsy.

But I knew he saw me . . . and I knew that *he* knew I could see him!

If you can see them, they'll know it, Lina had warned. *But you should be able to outrun them . . . .*

I couldn't run home, because the ghoul was blocking my way. So, I ran in the opposite direction, down the block. I might have screamed, but I don't remember. All I knew was that I wanted to get away from that thing!

My sneakers pounded the sidewalk. While I ran, I managed a quick glance over my shoulder. The creature was still lumbering along, and there was no doubt about it: he was coming after me.

But I was outrunning him. He appeared to be running, sort of. But he was so bulky that it seemed like he was having a difficult time. Thankfully, he couldn't run as fast as I could.

Think, Ashlynn, think! my mind screamed as I ran. *Think!*

I tried to remember everything that Lina had told me about the ghouls, but nothing came to mind. All she'd said was that she'd tell me later.

And I couldn't help but remember how worried she'd looked.

Why? What was it about the creatures that had made her so concerned?

No matter, now. I had to concentrate on getting away from the beast.

I turned suddenly, and cut between two houses. My plan was to run home by dashing through backyards. After all, the ghoul was slower than me. I should be able to outrun him.

That's when I saw Mr. Harris, another one of our neighbors. He's really nice. He was in his backyard, repairing his lawnmower. The mower was on its side, and Mr. Harris was kneeling in the grass, holding a screwdriver.

"Mr. Harris!" I shouted, and he turned. I ran up to him. "Mr. Harris! There's a creature after me!"

Mr. Harris looked concerned. He stood up, and I pointed. "He'll be coming around the side of the house any second now!"

But he didn't.

My heart thundered, and my breathing was heavy. I was shaking.

More seconds ticked past.

"What did you say was after you?" Mr. Harris asked. He sounded concerned, but he also sounded like he didn't believe me.

"Some . . . some *creature*," I stammered. "He was right behind me!"

Mr. Harris backtracked my path around the side of the house. I followed, but at a distance.

There was no sign of the ghoul!

Mr. Harris walked back toward me. "You young people these days," he said with a smile and a wave of his screwdriver. "You imagine too many things."

Imagining things?!?! I thought. *I know what I saw!*

But, then again, I'm the only one who can see the wood elves. Maybe I'm the only one who can see the ghouls, too.

And if that was the case, I wanted to get home, and quick. Hopefully, Lina would come and tell me more about the ghouls.

"Well, I really *thought* I saw a creature," I told Mr. Harris. "I really did."

Actually, I *know* I did . . . but it would have been useless to tell Mr. Harris, since I knew he wouldn't believe me.

"With an imagination like that, you ought to write books," Mr. Harris said, and he returned to repairing his lawnmower.

"Well, thanks anyway," I said, and continued walking. I could see my house in the distance, and I decided to keep cutting through the backyards until I was home. After all . . . I had no idea where that ghoul was. The quicker I made it home, the better.

Unfortunately, the ghoul had other plans for me . . . .

7

I walked quickly, cautiously, looking all around, searching for any sign of the mysterious, strange creature. Thoughts whirled in my head like a twisting tornado.

What are those things? I wondered. *Where did they come from? Can anyone else see them? Are they dangerous?*

Lina would have the answers, I was certain. I sure hoped I would see her soon!

The sky was stale and gray, but there were a few pieces of blue behind the puffy clouds. I sure would be glad when it got warmer. I like the winter and spring in Grand Rapids, but summer is my favorite season.

I made it through one yard. In a house, I saw a figure of a woman at a window. She waved when she saw me, and I waved back. People on our block are like that: we may not know one another very well, but everyone is friendly.

Only three more yards. Now I could see our house clearly, and I felt more and more relieved with every step I took.

But my mind kept going back to that hideous creature that came after me. It had to have been one of the ghouls Lina had mentioned. I shuddered, remembering its enormous size, giant head, and huge, dark teeth. Whatever the thing was, he should really see a dentist.

Only one more backyard to cut through, and I would be home. What a relief. I planned to go right to my bedroom and start my homework assignments, hoping Lina would soon show up and explain everything.

Suddenly, I was overcome with fear. It was so strong that I stopped walking and looked around. I don't know why I was so freaked out, because there was nothing around that looked frightening. Everything was normal, and I didn't see anything out of the ordinary.

Until—

Ahead of me, in the grass, something moved. It was in my backyard, not far from our house.

My fear grew. I felt dizzy.

Something was coming up from the ground in our backyard!

My fear ballooned inside me as I realized that a ghoul was taking shape, right before my eyes! *He was coming up from the ground!*

And what was even weirder: the grass and ground were undisturbed. You would think if something that big was coming out of the ground, the lawn would be torn up.

Not so. The creature rose up like mist, until he was all the way out of the ground. He looked sort of like a ghost, but after he was all the way up out of the ground, his features grew thick and dense. He looked horrid.

But, as it was, luck was on my side this time. The creature had emerged from the ground not twenty feet from where I stood . . . and he was facing the other way! He couldn't see me . . . yet.

I had to think fast. If he turned he would see me for sure.

Should I turn and run in the other direction? Would I be able to outrun him?

Not far away was a spruce tree. Its limbs were thick and dense, filled with spiny needles. Sometimes, when I play hide and seek with my friends, I'll tuck down on the ground and crawl within the branches. It makes a great hiding place.

It would be easier to hide than to run away, I thought. The spruce was only a few feet from me, and I could be there in seconds.

Of course, if the ghoul spotted me, I'd have to run anyway. But if I could hide within the thick spruce branches, maybe I could watch the ghoul and see what he did.

I quickly sidestepped to the tree. My eyes never left the ghoul, which hadn't turned around. He seemed to be looking at something on the far side of our house. I fell to the ground quietly, and slipped between the branches. The sharp, prickly needles poked at me, but I hardly noticed. I crawled within the dense limbs, nestling close to the trunk.

There, I thought. *I can see him, but I don't think he can see me.* I felt a little better, knowing I was out of sight.

But that thing came straight out of the ground! I thought. *How can that be?* It didn't tear up the grass or ground, but, rather, rose from the earth like a dark ghost.

The ghoul began to move. He stumbled toward our house, and had to lean down to peer in through the window. My mom was in there, somewhere, and I knew that she would totally freak if she saw the thing.

But if she *did* see it, at least she would be able to use the telephone and call the police! Maybe they could catch the creature.

I heard a sharp, familiar bouncing noise—*boing! boing! boing!* —echoing from the front of our house, and I recognized it immediately as a basketball dribbling on pavement. My brother, probably, home from basketball practice. Rick did the same thing every day: he dribbled the ball up the driveway, put it away in the garage, and walked into the house.

But he didn't do that today.

Instead, he appeared at the side of the house, carrying his backpack and his basketball.

My brother was coming into the backyard!

How could I warn him in time? What could I do? He had no idea there was a huge creature only a few feet from the house!

While I fretted and wondered what to do, Rick strode along the side of our house, whistling as if he didn't have a care in the world. And he probably didn't.

At least, not yet.

Because, at that very moment, the ghoul heard him.

The beast turned.

Rick rounded the corner, and was now in clear view of the gigantic ghoul.

It raised its arms high and wide.

There was nothing I could do. My brother wasn't even going to have a chance to defend himself.

9

Rick stopped.

The creature held his position, like a huge bear preparing to lunge.

My brother glanced around the backyard, like he was looking for something.

He can't see the ghoul! I thought. *Just like he can't see Lina, Deepo, or Mirak!*

The question was: would the ghoul do anything? It was obvious the creature could see

Rick, but I was equally sure Rick couldn't see the creature.

Whatever Rick was looking for in the backyard, he didn't find it. He turned and walked away, completely unaware of the hideous ghoul that had only been a few feet from him. He disappeared around the front of the house, and I heard the *boing! boing! boing!* of the basketball on pavement. Then, I heard the front door open and close.

Meanwhile, the ghoul had started walking, heading into our neighbor's yard. What a relief. The farther he was from me, the better.

I watched him continue through a few more yards. I'm sure no one could see him. If they could, they'd probably start screaming. The creature even walked right past Mr. Harris, who was still repairing his lawnmower! He never saw the ghoul, and the creature didn't bother Mr. Harris.

When I could no longer see the ghoul, I slipped out from my hiding place. Needles scratched at my face as I crawled to my feet.

"Lina, where are you?" I whispered. Lina would have the answers, I was sure. Of course, I wasn't sure I wanted to know the truth about the ghouls. After all, Lina seemed to be afraid of them.

I bolted to the front of the house, sprinted onto the porch, and went inside. Rick had already plopped down on the sofa, and he was watching television. Mom was at the dining room table, working. She works for the newspaper, and she's able to work at home a few days a week. She looked up when I came into the kitchen.

"Ashlynn," she said, taking off her glasses. "You look as white as a ghost. Are you feeling all right?"

"Yeah," I said. "I'm fine."

I wondered if I should tell her about the ghoul. She would probably think I was going crazy! I figured that, at least for the time being, I wouldn't say anything.

"How was school today?" Mom asked.

"Oh, the usual," I replied. "Lots of homework. I think I'm going to get started."

"Are you sure you're feeling okay?" Mom asked again.

"Yeah, I'm fine," I said. "Really, I am. I just need to get started on my homework."

I turned, walked down the hall, and went into my bedroom. I looked out the window as a car went by on the street.

Suddenly, Lina appeared on the windowsill! I don't think I've ever been happier to see her!

I closed my bedroom door, went to the window, and slid it open. Then, I slid back the screen, and Lina hopped inside and sat on the edge of the sill. I closed the window.

"I am *so* glad to see you!" I said anxiously. "I saw some of those . . . those *things!*"

Lina nodded, and her wings fluttered. "I know," she said. "I'm sorry I didn't have time to explain before. Now, I can. It's time you learned the truth."

"The truth?" I replied. "The truth about what?"

Something inside me told me I didn't want to know. I knew Lina was probably going to tell me some horrifying secret, something that would probably give me nightmares.

And, as it turned out, I was right.

10

"There is much you don't know about Grand Rapids," Lina said. "You know about us, and you know that you are special, because you can see us. Very few people can, you know."

"But why?" I asked. "Why am I special?"

Lina shook her head, and she fluttered into the air and lit on my dresser, where she sat with her legs dangling over the edge. "I don't know," she said. "But some humans are able to see us. Very few, however. We don't know how many."

"So, where did the ghouls come from?" I asked. "You never told me about those before."

"There is a lot you don't know about the city," Lina said. "And there is a lot to know about the ghouls, but I will try to keep it short, and explain only what you need to know. The ghouls have been here for a long, long time. However, they live in secret caverns, deep in the ground. I've never told you about the ghouls or the caverns because I didn't want you to worry. Besides, a long time ago, with the help of two humans like you, we used magic to banish the ghouls from coming to the surface. You see, we wood elves lose all our powers if we travel beneath the ground. Years ago, with the help of two humans who could see us, we were able to use our magic to stop the ghouls. We thought they were gone for good, but now we know the magic is wearing off."

"I saw one come up out of the ground!" I exclaimed. "Right in our backyard! And I think one of them tore a hole in Mrs. Walker's fence!"

Lina nodded. "They can appear at any time, in any place around the city," she said. "They are of no danger to most people. Not yet, anyway."

"What do you mean 'most' people?" I asked.

"As you know, most people can't see us," Lina answered, "and they can't see the ghouls. The ghouls know this, so they don't worry about anyone that cannot see them. Only those who know of their existence—those who can see them—pose a danger to them."

I was confused. "But I can see the ghouls, just like I can see you," I said. "How am I a danger to them?"

"Because you have the power to stop them, and they know it," Lina replied flatly. "You see, years ago, we used magic to keep the ghouls from coming to the surface. Some of them—the more powerful ones—have the ability to take over the body of a human being. However, it's not easy for them. Usually, when they try to take over a human, they don't succeed . . . at first. But after a while, they get good at it . . . just like anything else."

"It just takes practice," I said, my voice quaking.

Lina nodded. "That's right," she agreed. "And that's what the ghouls want to do. Once they begin to take over the bodies of humans, they will have super-human powers."

Suddenly, there was a knock on my bedroom door.

"Ashlynn?" It was my mom.

"Yes?"

My bedroom door opened, and Mom poked her head in. "Are you on the phone?" she asked.

"Um, no," I replied.

"I thought I heard you talking to someone."

"No," I replied, shaking my head. Then, thinking quickly, I pointed to a pile of papers and textbooks on the bed: "I was just reading my homework out loud."

"Oh, okay. Dinner will be ready in a little while."

"Thanks, Mom."

She closed the door, and I turned to Lina.

"What do you mean, 'stop them'?" I asked Lina.

"Exactly that," Lina replied. "Only those who see them will be able to stop them. After all . . . if you can't see something, how can you stop it?"

I remembered a scary book I'd read not long ago. It was about a girl in Illinois who had terrible problems with invisible iguanas. She had a hard time in the book, because she couldn't see the iguanas. I figured the guy who wrote the book had a weird imagination.

"I'm not going to do anything to stop them," I said. "I'm just going to stay out of their way and leave them alone."

Lina looked at me with deepening worry. "Just because you leave *them* alone doesn't mean they'll leave *you* alone, Ashlynn."

That worried me . . . a *lot*.

Later that night . . . .

After finishing dinner and my homework, I went to the kitchen, got a glass of water, and said good-night to Mom and Dad. Then, I went back to my room, placed the glass of water on my night stand, changed into my nightgown, and crawled beneath the covers.

I had been laying in bed for a long time, but I couldn't sleep. I'd gone to bed early, so it wasn't late, but I just tossed and turned in my bed.

Earlier, when Lina was still here, Deepo and Mirak had shown up. They're usually pretty funny, but tonight they had been very serious. They told me they'd explain more tomorrow, that the ghouls were planning something and they didn't know what it was.

It was all very scary. The image of that creepy ghoul coming up out of the ground kept coming back to me again and again, and I realized how strange everything seemed. It occurred to me that most kids my age have a pretty normal life . . . but since I could actually see the wood elves and the ghouls, I was different from everyone else.

Before, I used to think it was cool.

Now, I didn't think so. Now, I just wanted to be a normal girl. I didn't want to have to worry about creatures coming up from the ground and chasing after me.

In fact, even in my bedroom, I didn't feel safe. I left my closet door open, and I wondered if there was a ghoul hidden in the deep, cavernous shadow. I put my school clothing for the next day on a chair near my dresser, and its silhouette looked like a huge ghoul sitting there, waiting for me to go to sleep. It was silly, I know . . . but it still creeped me out.

And I sat up in bed every so often to look outside, expecting to see one of those hideous things in the yard, wandering around, looking for me.

If I saw one, and he saw me, what would he do? More important, what would *I* do?

I didn't even want to think about it.

I sure wish I knew more about what's going on, I thought. *I wish Lina, Deepo, and Mirak would have told me more.*

The shadow of my coat hanging on the back of my door gave me a start: it reminded me of a ghoul.

"This is crazy," I whispered. *"I'm never going to get any sleep."*

I closed my eyes . . . but I opened them when I heard a noise. It was very faint, and, at first, I thought it was a bug on the window. Once in a while, a beetle will make a scratching noise when its wings flutter against the screen.

But when I saw the shadow on the opposite wall of my bedroom, I knew the noise hadn't been created by any bug or beetle.

On the wall was the shadow of two giant, fat hands!

Which meant—

I turned . . . only to see a pair of hands pressed against my window!

In the splint second before I was going to start screaming my head off, I realized the hands didn't belong to a ghoul . . . but to my friend, Darius Perry! I couldn't see his face, but I recognized his signal. You see, sometimes Darius needs help with his homework. When he does, he'll come over and tap on my screen three times.

I stood up, went to the window, and slid it open.

"Darius!" I hissed through the screen. *"You scared me!"*

"I'm scared, too!" he replied.

"Why?" I asked.

"Because I didn't finish all of my math homework!" he answered, and he unrolled the homework papers he'd tucked beneath his arm.

I rolled my eyes. *"Are you kidding me?!?! You scared me half to death to tell me that?!?!"*

"Well, you always said that if I needed help with my homework, you would help me," Darius said.

"Yeah, but it's bedtime," I replied. *"I'll help you in the morning."*

"Oh, all right," Darius whispered. *"I'll see you in the morning, before class."*

"Good night," I said. Darius turned, and I watched him sprint across the lawn and across the street. He vanished in a jumble of shadows, and I closed my bedroom window and crawled back into bed. Then, I giggled. I couldn't believe I'd been so scared by Darius!

But, then again, the shadow of his arms on the wall *did* look huge. They *did* look like they could have been the arms of a ghoul.

Ghoul.

It seemed odd to even *think* the word. Yet, now I couldn't get it out of my mind. I couldn't help but to think of those giant, hideous things wandering around outside.

Maybe even right now, while I was tucked in bed.

And could they get inside the house? I wished I'd asked Lina that question. If they could, that meant I wouldn't be safe in my own house, in my own room.

I looked at the dark shadows in my closet, and the silhouette of my clothing on the back of the chair.

Ghouls. Right here, in Grand Rapids.

I closed my eyes, determined to get to sleep. It would do me no good to worry about it anymore tonight.

And I'd almost succeeded in sleeping. I was dozing off, almost asleep, when I heard a scream that pierced the night.

I snapped up in bed, my heart pounding, as the shriek died away. The scream had come from inside our house, I was sure.

Then, it came again! Except, this time, it didn't stop. Someone in our house was screaming, and I recognized the voice.

Mom!

I was so scared I couldn't get out of bed.

What could make Mom scream like that?!?! I wondered, but I already knew the answer.

If Mom saw one of those ghouls, that would make her scream. That would scare her senseless!

In addition to Mom's screams, I could now hear more commotion. There were banging sounds, and my dad shouted something. Mom stopped screaming, and then I heard Dad laugh a little.

I got up, walked to my bedroom door, and opened it a tiny bit . . . just as the hall light came on. I poked my head out.

Rick, too, was at his bedroom door, peering out, just as Dad came around the corner, wearing his pajamas. Dad's pajamas have little blue bunnies printed all over. They make him look really silly, but he says he doesn't care.

"Don't worry," Dad said, glancing at Rick and then to me. He grinned sleepily. "A bat got into the house and was flying around our room. Your mother freaked out, but I was able to open the window and shoo it outside."

Talk about relief! For a minute, I thought a ghoul had gotten inside our house!

I closed my bedroom door and went back to bed, wishing I had more answers. Wishing that Lina was here. I always felt better when she was around.

But I would have to wait.

And finally, I was able to drift off to sleep. I'm not sure when, but I don't think it took long.

What I do remember was waking up in the middle of the night. The clock on my dresser said it was nearly four in the morning.

I sat up, leaned over, and picked up my glass of water, put it to my lips, and took a sip.

And as I looked around my room, I could see ghouls everywhere . . . in my mind, of course. I knew it was only my imagination, but I couldn't help it. There was a ghoul in my closet, one in my chair, and one at my bedroom door. In my mind, they were everywhere.

I took another sip of water.

A movement caught my eye. Something outside.

A chill iced through my veins, and my skin crawled. My heart trip-hammered in my chest.

Slowly—ever so slowly—I turned my head and looked out the window.

There, in our front yard, in the hazy, bluish-white glow of the streetlight, stood a ghoul! He was enormous, and his shadow ballooned over the lawn like a dark cloud.

I blinked hard. I knew I was dreaming, and I needed to wake up.

But when I opened my eyes, the ghoul was still there!

I was shaking so badly that I nearly spilled my water. I placed it on my night stand, nearly dropping it in the process. The glass made a loud *clunk* as I set it down.

The ghoul was still in the yard. I don't think he could see me, but I sure could see him!

Then, I tried one last thing. I pinched myself—hard, too—on the arm. I figured that would wake me up.

Nope. I was already awake.

Which meant there really *was* a ghoul in our front yard, at that very moment!

And as I wondered what I should do, the ghoul turned. He turned, and looked right at me.

Then, he started walking toward my window!

I couldn't scream, and I knew it wouldn't do any good if I did. I knew Mom and Dad would come running, but when I tried to explain there was a ghoul in the yard, they would just tell me I was having a nightmare.

Meanwhile, the ghoul was getting closer and closer, walking toward my window with slow, zombie-like movements. His arms were raised, like he was reaching for me.

What do I do?!?! What do I do?!?! What do I do?!?! My mind was racing a mile a minute. Faster, even.

The ghoul was right at my window now, peering inside. He was, by far, the ugliest, creepiest creature I had ever seen in my life, and the velvety shadows in the yard made the scene look like something out of a scary movie. What was he going to do? Could he get inside? Would he try? If he did, he was bound to make a lot of noise. Mom and Dad would hear the ruckus for sure, and come running.

That made me feel a *little* better. Not much, though, since the ghoul was still at my window.

So I bit my lip and closed my eyes. *Hard.* I kept them closed for a long time.

When I open my eyes, he'll be gone, I told myself over and over.

I don't know how long I kept my eyes closed. A couple of minutes, at least.

And when I opened them, the ghoul was gone! *Whew!*

I craned my neck and scanned the yard for any sign of the creature, but I didn't see him. Maybe he went away, or sank back into the ground.

I didn't know, and I didn't care. The only thing that mattered was that he was gone.

Could it only have been my imagination? I wondered. *Was it just my mind playing tricks on me? Maybe I only* thought *I saw the ghoul.*

No, that wasn't the case. After all, I'd pinched myself. That should have woken me up, if I'd been dreaming or imagining things.

I sat up for another few minutes, then I got up and closed the curtain. If another ghoul showed up, I didn't want to see him.

And I fell asleep again . . . only to be awakened a short time later by a noise at the windowsill.

This time, thankfully, it was Lina . . . but she didn't have good news . . . .

15

When I awoke in the morning, Dad had already left for work. Like always, Mom had packed my lunch box the night before and placed it in the fridge. Now, it was on the kitchen counter. She had already started her work for the day, and was studying several sheets of paper laid out on the table.

"See you later, Mom," I said. "Thanks for lunch."

"You're welcome," she replied, and gave me a curious look. "Are you all right, Ashlynn?" she asked. "You look tired."

"I . . . I guess I didn't sleep real well," I replied.

Mom smiled. "You and me both," she said, "with that awful bat flying around our room. I'm glad your father was able to get it to fly out the window."

I managed a weak smile, picked up my lunch box, and headed for the bus stop. As I walked, I thought about what Lina had told me when she'd come to my window in the early morning hours.

Deepo and Mirak are missing.

That's what she'd said.

Lina told me that she and the other wood elves were very worried. She hadn't seen Deepo or Mirak since the day before, when they came to my window. No one knew where they were, and that wasn't like them at all.

Deepo and Mirak are missing.

True, I never saw them very much. It was Lina who usually came to my window a few days a week. Deepo's and Mirak's visits were far less frequent. Still, they were friends, and I was worried, too. I hoped that something hadn't happened to them.

"What can I do?" I had asked Lina.

"Just keep your eyes out for them," she told me. "We're not sure where they are, but we don't think the ghouls have anything to do with it. We think that Deepo and Mirak are planning something . . . something that might stop the ghouls once and for all."

"Like what?" I asked.

Lina shook her head, shrugged, and fluttered her wings. "We don't know. But what they might be planning could be dangerous . . . so maybe they thought they would do it on their own, so no one else would get hurt. We don't know this for sure, though."

"I saw one of those creepy ghouls a while ago," I told Lina. "He came right up to my window!"

Lina nodded, as if this was to be expected. "Just remember what I told you, Ashlynn . . . you are faster than they are. You should be able to outrun them, if one comes after you. Stay as far away from them as you can, and you should be all right."

I was a little relieved to hear her say that. Knowing I had a chance against those ugly things made me feel better.

Not much . . . but a little, at least.

"Just go to school like you normally do," she'd said. "I'll come by later today. There's more I have to tell you. But be careful. The ghouls know you can see them."

A bat suddenly flew by the window, and its wings made a flapping sound, crinkling, like wax paper . . . which I thought was strange. I've seen lots of bats, and some of them have flown right by my head. But their wings don't make any sound at all.

The reason? It wasn't a bat, after all! It was another wood elf! He hovered by the window, not far from Lina. In all my years, I'd never seen any other wood elves besides Lina, Deepo, and Mirak.

Lina explained it was because most wood elves don't like to be around people.

"Lina!" the wood elf exclaimed. "Come quick! It's important!"

Lina flitted off the windowsill and into the air.

"Wait!" I hissed. "Tell me more about the ghouls!"

"Later today!" Lina exclaimed. "I'll be back!" Then, she vanished into the sky with the other wood elf, zipping away like two speeding dragonflies.

Gee, I thought. *Other kids worry about getting bad grades and stuff like that. I have to worry about ghouls. It's not fair.*

I walked warily to the bus stop, my eyes twitching back and forth, on constant ghoul-watch. If one appeared, I wanted to be able to get away from it . . . which meant that I'd have to spot the creature before he spotted me.

Thankfully, I didn't see any as I made my way to the bus stop. As I waited with the other kids, I didn't say much. Oh, I knew most of them . . . but

I just wasn't in a talkative mood. I just nodded and said 'good morning' to everyone. My brother Rick was a little late, and he came running up just as the bus arrived.

And I was relieved. I knew that once I was on the bus, once I was safely nestled at my desk in class, I'd be safe.

Or, at least, I *thought* I would be.

Not so.

In fact, I was about to find out more than I ever wanted to know about the gruesome ghouls of Grand Rapids . . . and what they were up to!

16

Before I went to class, I met Darius in the cafeteria and helped him with his math homework. He finally caught on, and finished his assignment only minutes before the bell rang.

"Next time, pay attention to the teacher," I smirked.

"Hey, I would have been able to get it done last night," he replied, "if I hadn't spent so much time looking for my softball."

"Did you find it?" I asked.

"No," he said. "It's no big deal, really."

We walked to class together. Darius is a really good friend, and there have been several times over the past few years that I'd thought about telling him about the wood elves. But I never did, because I knew he would think I was crazy.

Which was a bummer, because I didn't have anyone to talk to about what was going on.

Class wasn't very exciting. We graded each other's math papers, and I only got two wrong out of 40 problems. Darius got five wrong, but he thought that was pretty good . . . considering he'd just barely had enough time to get the assignment done for class.

"You know," he said to me during lunchtime, "I've been meaning to talk to you about something. But you have to promise not to tell anyone."

"Sure," I said, setting my lunch box on the table. The cafeteria is big, with lots of folding tables. There were a lot of other students around, but we were sitting alone.

"I mean . . . this is going to sound really weird," he continued. "You might think I'm crazy."

Darius, I thought, *nothing can be weirder than wood elves and ghouls that no one else can see but myself.*

"I won't think you're crazy," I said, opening my lunch box. "I promise."

He looked around to make sure no other classmates could overhear. At that very same moment, I reached into my lunch box and got the shock of my life.

Deepo and Mirak were in my lunch box!

I was so surprised I nearly gasped out loud! Imagine opening your lunch box, expecting to find a sandwich and a snack, but, instead, seeing two small, living creatures!

I quickly composed myself, hoping Darius didn't see my shocked expression. I was going to close the lunch box, but I knew no one else could see the two wood elves.

80

Deepo and Mirak are quite comical. Whenever I see them, they're joking playfully with each other. The look just like Lina, but they're boys. Men, actually. Deepo has a full, thick beard and mustache. Mirak is sort of short and squatty. Neither of them are taller than a pencil. And they both have wings, of course, just like Lina.

Both of them stood up and stretched. They probably needed it, being that they'd been crammed into my lunch box for who knows how long.

When they stood, however, Darius's eyes swelled like ping pong balls, and his mouth hung open. He nearly fell off his chair, and his hand shot out, a single finger, pointing at the two wood elves.

He could see them!

"There they are!" he exclaimed, as he jumped up from the lunch table and took a step back. "They're right there! On the table!"

Students were looking at us. Some had stopped eating and were staring.

"Shhhh!" I said. *"People are watching! Sit down!"*

Up until then, I thought no one else could see the wood elves but me. I was amazed to find out Darius could see them, too!

He sat down, but he kept looking at Deepo and Mirak, who had stepped out of the lunch box and were standing on the table. I looked around. Some students were still staring at Darius and me.

"Yes, you're right, Darius," I said, plucking my sandwich and a banana from my lunch box. I held them up and looked at him. "My sandwich and my banana are right here." I said it very matter-of-factly, for the benefit of the students who had watched Darius's strange behavior. Some students shook their heads. Some of them made some whispering comments, but they all stopped looking at us.

Now I had a problem. I wanted to talk to Deepo and Mirak, but I didn't want anyone looking at me and thinking I was talking to my lunch box!

And I wanted to talk to Darius, too, to find out how long he'd been able to see the wood elves. I could probably explain a few things to him, since he probably thought he was going crazy!

"They are *real!"* Darius hissed. *"The green fairies* are *real!"*

Hearing this, Deepo and Mirak became angry.

"Who are you calling 'fairies'?" Deepo demanded, jamming his clenched fist to his waist. His wings fluttered and he flew into the air, hovering right in front of Darius's face. "I'll have you know that fairies are pink and red, and look nothing at all like us. In fact, there aren't even any fairies around here!"

"Deepo, please," I said. "He didn't mean to hurt your feelings. He's confused, that's all."

"I'll say," Darius said. His eyes were still huge, and his mouth was still open in a silent gape.

"Guys," I said quietly, "we have to be very careful as we speak. Darius, you and I have to look at each other when we talk. Deepo and Mirak: I need to talk to you, too, but when I do, I'll need to look at Darius, so no one around will think I'm talking to my lunch box."

"You know them by *name?*" Darius said, a bit too loudly. Some students looked at us, then looked away.

"Shhh, yes, just keep your voice down," I said. "Keep your voice down, and I'll explain."

Mirak spoke. "Let us go first, Ashlynn," he said urgently. "There are some things you need to know about the ghouls."

"Ghouls?!?!" Darius gasped. Again, students turned their heads.

"Shhhhh!" I hissed to Darius.

"Sorry," Darius replied. He glanced down at the two wood elves like they were poisonous snakes about to strike.

Mirak started to speak. "The ghouls are—"

Just then, Mr. Hoffman strode into the lunchroom. Mr. Hoffman is the principal. He's very nice, but he wears strange neckties that are all sorts of different colors.

He called out someone's name, and waggled his finger. A student—I don't know who it was—stood up and started walking toward Mr. Hoffman. He was probably in some sort of trouble.

But then I realized that we might *all* be in trouble . . . because Mr. Hoffman was no longer Mr. Hoffman!

Right before our eyes, he turned into a ghoul!

In a split-second, the ghoul was gone, and in his place stood Mr. Hoffman.

But I knew what I saw. So did Deepo and Mirak. Darius was looking at me, so he hadn't seen it.

I looked down at Deepo and Mirak, then quickly looked up at Darius.

"That's what we needed to tell you," Deepo said grimly. "The ghouls are trying to take over humans."

"That's what Lina told me," I said.

"They're trying, but they don't have enough power to do it, yet," Mirak said. "But they will, soon. The person they take over doesn't even know it. We're seeing it happen all around Grand Rapids. They aren't powerful enough to completely take over a human, but it won't be long before they are."

"But why are they doing it?" I asked.

"We don't know for sure just yet," Deepo replied. "But they tried, years ago, to do the same thing. With the help of two humans, we were able to stop them." He and Mirak flew into the air and hovered in the space between Darius and me. That made it easier to look at them while we spoke, without any students thinking we were crazy. If anyone was looking, it would appear that I was talking to Darius . . . unless they could hear me talking about ghouls and wood elves! Then, I'd be the talk of the school. Everyone would think that I, Ashlynn Meyer, had gone completely koo-koo!

"Lina says that everyone is looking for you," I said to Deepo and Mirak. "And what were you doing in my lunch box?"

Deepo looked at Mirak, fluttering in the air only a few inches away. "It was *his* fault," he said, pointing an accusing finger.

Mirak shook his head in defiance. "No, it was your fault, too, Deepo," he replied sharply.

"I can't believe I'm seeing and hearing this," Darius said. Deepo and Mirak ignored him.

"It was *your* idea to eat her granola bar!" Deepo fumed.

"Maybe so," Mirak said, "but it was *your* idea to eat the *whole thing!*"

I looked in my lunch box. Sure enough, the only thing left of my granola bar was the wrapper and a few crumbs.

"Thanks, guys," I said sarcastically. "But how did you get stuck in the lunch box?"

Deepo pointed at Mirak. "Ninny, here, wouldn't leave without finishing the granola bar. When your mom came by, we both had to cover the wrapper with the sandwich, so she wouldn't see that someone had eaten it. We were still in your lunch box when she closed the lid and flipped the latch. We were trapped all night long!"

"Serves you right for eating my granola bar," I said with a thin grin. I really wasn't all that mad. Besides, it seemed kind of funny. I could imagine them stuck in my lunch box, trying to figure a way to get out. They probably argued with each other all night!

"Lina thought that you guys were coming up with a secret plan to stop the ghouls," I said.

Deepo and Mirak shook their heads.

"No," Mirak said. "All we've been doing is trying to figure out how to get out of your lunch box."

"After we ate your granola bar, of course," Deepo replied. Then he burped, and I laughed out loud.

Darius was still watching, his eyes as wide as saucers, his mouth still agape. He looked more confused than ever.

"None of that matters now," Mirak said. "What matters is stopping the ghouls."

All of this is going to mean big trouble, I thought.

And very soon, I would be proven right.

19

"Okay," Darius said to me as we walked. "Run that by me again."

The bus had just dropped us off, and we were on our way home. I had just told Darius everything I knew about the wood elves and the ghouls. Of course, I didn't know all that much about the ghouls, but I told him what Lina had told me. I hadn't had a chance to talk to him about it during school, and there were too many other kids around on the bus.

"I first saw the wood elves when I was real little," I said. "That's when I met Lina. At first, I told my mom and dad about them. But they didn't believe me. So, I decided to keep it a secret. Lina and I have been friends ever since. You've already met Deepo and Mirak, in the lunchroom today. I just wish we'd had more time to talk to them."

"And they live in the forest?" Darius asked.

"Yes," I replied, "but I don't know where. Lina says their city is at the top of a tall tree. I've never been there, but Lina says that it's not far."

But before I continued explaining, I had some questions for Darius.

"When did you first see a wood elf?" I asked.

"Last year," he replied. "At first, I thought it was a bird. He was right by the porch, when I was sitting outside. When he saw me looking at him, he flew off."

"And you didn't tell anyone?"

Darius stopped walking, and I did, too.

"Are you *kidding?!?!*" he replied. "People would've thought I was out of my mind! In fact, I thought I was going crazy . . . until I saw another one a couple of weeks later."

"That's why I never said anything to anyone," I replied. "I didn't want anyone to think I was cracking up. Mom and Dad just thought that Lina was my imaginary friend. They didn't believe me when I told them about the wood elves, so I just gave up trying to explain that they were real."

We started walking again, slowly. "But what did those two dudes say about stopping the ghouls?" Darius asked.

"They're not 'dudes'," I replied. "Their names are Deepo and Mirak. And they think they've found a way to stop the ghouls."

Deepo and Mirak wanted to explain more while we were in the lunchroom, but we ran out of time. They told me they'd find Lina, and come to my house later that evening.

"Tell me more about those ghouls," Darius said. "I haven't seen any of them yet. Where did they come from?"

His timing couldn't have been worse. Just as I opened my mouth to tell him what a ghoul looks like, one came up from the ground . . . right in front of us!

20

"Darius! Run!" I shrieked, and we both turned and started running as fast as we could. It was hard, though, because I had a backpack filled with books and my empty lunch box. Darius dropped his books, and they scattered all over the grass beneath a tree.

"The ghouls can't move very fast!" I told Darius as we sprinted down the street. There were a few other kids around, and they gave us strange looks.

Of course, they couldn't see the ghouls, or else they would be running, too.

I looked back over my shoulder. This ghoul was a little faster than the others, and it was taking us longer to get away from him.

Our chances will be better if we try to hide, I thought.

"Over this way!" I ordered Darius, and he followed me as I cut across a lawn to the side of a big, white, two-story house. All the curtains were drawn, and it didn't appear there was anyone home.

Best of all, there was a row of tall, thick shrubs growing along the side of the house. If we could make it there without the ghoul seeing us, it would be the perfect place to hide.

"There!" I pointed, and Darius and I pushed through the branches and limbs. They were scratchy and some of them stung, but I hardly noticed the pain.

We knelt down on the cool ground, tucked within the dense, tightly-knitted leaves. I dropped my backpack and lunch box and pushed them aside. Darius and I were both gasping for breath. My heart thunked madly beneath my ribs.

And we'd made it to our hiding place just in time, too . . . because it wasn't long before we spotted the ghoul. He was hard to see, because the branches and leaves were so thick. The creature was on the sidewalk, but he must've seen us run across the grass toward the side of the house. He turned and began coming our way.

"I hope we're doing the right thing," Darius said in a trembling whisper.

"Just don't say anything, and don't move," I replied quietly. *"I don't think he can see us."*

I could see movement through the branches, and I knew he was getting closer. I could only hope that he continued walking past the house, and into the backyard.

The movement stopped not far from where we were hiding. A lump grew in my throat, and I could feel it getting bigger and bigger. I swallowed hard, and made a sound like a gulping bullfrog.

The creature approached the bushes. My heart skipped a beat, then began thrashing. Darius closed his eyes hard.

Please don't find us, I thought, knowing that, if the ghoul discovered where we were hiding, at least one of us wouldn't be getting away. Lina said that the ghouls were slow, but if one of them got hold of you . . . .

Through the thick branches, I could see only slight movement. The creature was right next to the bushes! He was only a few feet away! I could even hear it breathing, in and out, in and out.

Please, please don't find us, I thought again.

But it was not to be.

Suddenly, two giant hands plunged violently into the shrubs!

21

I screamed and fell back against the house. I couldn't have run away if I tried. I was off balance, and the branches around me were too thick.

Next to me, Darius was so scared he fainted! He dropped to the ground, curled up, unconscious!

The hands pulled the branches apart, and the face of my brother appeared.

"What are you *doing* in there?" he asked.

I was so relieved I hung my head and let out a long, sighing gasp. It hadn't been a ghoul, after all.

Because the branches and leaves were so thick, I couldn't see very well. I'd only *thought* it was a ghoul. I was so glad it was only my brother.

But the ghoul that came up from the ground was still out there . . . somewhere.

"And what's up with him?" Rick said, pointing at Darius's motionless body on the ground. "Is he sick?"

"What are you doing here?!?!" I demanded. "What happened to the gh—"

But I stopped short. I knew Rick couldn't see the ghoul, and he would have thought I'd lost my marbles if I told him.

"I saw you and Darius running like Olympic sprinters," Rick said. "Darius dropped his books and left them scattered by a tree, so I thought something was wrong."

"I, uh, no, uh," I stammered. "Nothing's wrong. *What on earth was I going to tell him?*

Then, my mind ablaze with thoughts, I said: "We're just playing hide and seek with some friends." It wasn't the truth . . . but if I told him what we were *really* doing, he wouldn't believe me for a second!

"Ohhh," Darius groaned. He moved slightly, and he raised his head. "I'm awake, Mom," he slurred. "I'll be down for breakfast in a minute."

"Darius," I said, placing my hand on his shoulder and shaking him gently, "it's me . . . Ashlynn. Not your mother. And you're not at home, you're in the bushes, hiding."

"You guys are strange," Rick said, and he withdrew his hands. The limbs snapped back into place. "See you weirdos later," he said, and I could make out his shape through the shrubs as he walked away.

Next to me, Darius was coming to. "Wha . . . what happened?" he stuttered, sitting up. There was dirt on his cheek, and he reached up and wiped it away.

"You fainted," I said. "When those hands came through the bushes, we thought it was the ghoul. But it was only my brother."

"So, where's the ghoul, now?" Darius asked.

"You have leaves in your hair," I said, and I picked out a few dried, broken crisps from his knotty, black hair. "I have no idea where the ghoul is. But we'd better be extra careful."

I pulled some branches away and peered out. Not seeing the ghoul, I grasped the branches and used them to help pull me out. I looked around, still cautious.

No ghouls.

My backpack and lunch box were still on the ground, nestled in the bushes next to the house. I decided to leave them there, and come back after dinner to get them. Hopefully, it would be safer.

"Come on," I said to Darius, plunging my hand into the prickly branches. He grasped it, and I pulled him up and out.

"Man," he said, as he brushed himself off. "Yesterday, my biggest problems were homework and a lost softball. Today, it's ghouls and wood elves."

I shook my head. "The wood elves are our friends," I reminded him. "It's the ghouls we have to look out for. Come on . . . let's go pick up your books and go home. I can't wait to talk to Lina, Deepo, and Mirak tonight. Maybe they'll have a plan to stop the ghouls."

We started walking . . . and I realized that, even if the wood elves had a plan, it might already be too late . . . because when we turned and looked up the street, we saw ghouls.

Not one.

Not two.

Not *ten*.

Dozens of them. They were in yards, they were in the street. They were on the sidewalk, lumbering around like giant sloths.

Suddenly, one spotted us. He raised his hand and grunted an inhuman, beastly snarl.

All of the ghouls turned.

They stared . . . and began coming toward us.

"Darius," I said, my voice trembling. "I don't think we're going to be able to get your books and homework."

22

It was like something out of a movie—only worse.

I couldn't believe there were so many ghouls! They all looked pretty much the same. They were all about the same size, and all had similar facial features. The only thing that separated them was some had different clothing.

But one thing was certain: every single one looked absolutely horrifying!

"Let's get to the woods!" I shouted. *"There will be more places to hide!"*

We ran across lawns and headed toward the forest at the end of our block. I was familiar with the trails, and I was already thinking of places we might be able to hide. There were several big trees that had fallen down, and we might be able to hide behind their trunks. There were also a couple places where the brush was so thick that it was impossible to see through it.

And if we didn't find a place to hide? Well, we would just keep running along the trail. We could only hope we were faster than the ghouls.

Another thing that was very strange was there were people outside . . . and they were totally unaware of the rampaging ghouls. It seemed so weird that Darius and I were the only ones who could see them.

Mr. Harris was outside, trimming the hedges around his house. He saw us running.

"Well, you kids certainly are getting your exercise today," he said.

"Yep!" I huffed as we flew down the street. Mr. Harris continued working on his hedges, oblivious to the quickly approaching throng of ghouls.

We reached the end of our block and entered the forest. I was vaguely aware of the atmosphere darkening around us, because the forest is very thick. Later in the summer, when the leaves became even thicker and fuller, the forest stayed quite dark even during the day, as the heavily-leafed trees prevented most of the sunlight from shining through.

Our feet thumped on the damp, hard-packed trail. Darius was behind me as we ran, winding and zigzagging around trees. I had to raise my hands several times to knock branches out of our way. One sprang back and caught Darius in the chest unexpectedly, and he nearly fell.

"Sorry!" I yelled.

"Just keep going!" Darius shouted. "I don't want to get eaten by one of those chunky Frankenstein things!"

Behind us, I could hear branches snapping, and I knew the ghouls weren't too far away. Hopefully, they wouldn't be able to move very fast in the forest, simply because they were so big.

And while we ran, my eyes darted from side to side, searching for a place to hide. I knew we needed a place where we could be hidden on all sides, so even if the ghouls were all around us, we wouldn't be seen.

I got my wish.

Ahead of us, not far from the trail, was an enormous tree. While the tree itself didn't provide anyplace to hide, there was a large pile of brush right next to it. If we could wriggle beneath the branches, the ghouls might walk right past and not even know we were there!

"Right there!" I shouted, pointing at the brush pile. I left the trail and ran to the large gathering of dead branches. There seemed to be hundreds of branches . . . and that was our problem. There were just too many. They were so thick, there was no way we'd be able to crawl beneath them. It would take an hour to do it . . . and we didn't have more than sixty seconds!

We could hear branches snapping and popping as the ghouls lumbered through the forest. It sounded like they were all around us.

"What now?!?!" Darius asked. He was looking everywhere, panicking.

I looked around, too, desperately trying to find somewhere to go. Time was quickly running out.

More branches cracked and snapped. I was going to start running again, but I didn't know which direction to head. It seemed the ghouls were all around us, just out of sight.

And I knew they were getting closer with every passing second.

I looked at the huge tree looming above. It had a massive, fat trunk, but there were no low branches to grab ahold of. The top of the tree was thick with winding limbs that sprouted early, spring leaves. It would be a perfect place to hide . . . but there was no way to get there.

A ghoul appeared through the branches. Then another, and another. Everywhere we turned, we saw ghouls . . . and I realized we'd made a terrible mistake.

I swallowed hard.

"I'm sorry, Darius," I said. "I really thought we'd be able to get away."

Our luck had finally run out.

23

The ghouls began walking toward us. They had us trapped, and they knew it. They were stalking us like a pack of circling, hungry wolves, making their way to us without hurry. They knew there was nowhere we could go.

Darius, however, wasn't going to give up. He darted to the tree trunk and wrapped his arms around it—as much as he could, anyway. The trunk was far too big for him to reach all the way around. I knew he wasn't going to be able to climb two feet, but he tried. He jumped up, wrapped his arm around the trunk, and made attempts to shimmy up the tree . . . all in vain. There was nothing for him to grab, nothing to hold onto. He kept sliding back down.

Meanwhile, the ghouls were still coming for us. I looked for a place where I might be able to squirm between them, but couldn't find one. They were too big, and there were too many of them.

Suddenly, all the ghouls stopped. They had a curious expression on their faces. Some of them were looking up.

A small bird flew by my face, circling around and up. Then another. Two more.

And then I heard a voice I would recognize anywhere:

"Ashlynn!"

It was Lina! What I'd seen wasn't a bird . . . it was a wood elf!

I looked up to see dozens of wood elves buzzing all around, their wings beating the air, making plastic-flapping sounds. I couldn't tell which one was Lina, but I was glad to hear her voice.

"Both of you!" a wood elf ordered. "Hold your arms out to the side!"

"Huh?" Darius said as he failed at another attempt to climb the tree.

The ghouls started toward us again, growling and sneering, and making cow-like sounds. In fact, they probably smelled like cows, too. Creatures that ugly, I was sure, probably didn't smell like roses.

I snapped my arms straight out from my sides, where they were immediately swarmed by wood elves. There were at least a dozen at each arm, and I could feel them tugging at the sleeves of my sweatshirt.

"Do what they say, Darius!" I shouted. Darius looked at me, saw me holding my arms out, and did the same. Wood elves descended upon him, too, all along his arms and hands.

"Keep your arms out!" Lina piped shrilly, and I realized she was at the end of my right arm, just beneath my wrist.

The ghouls were only a few feet away. One of them reached out . . . and that's when I was pulled up and off the ground! I was suddenly airborne, yanked off my feet. Darius was, too . . . and just in time. A ghoul was so close to him that it managed to grab his foot.

"Let me go, you ugly moose!" he screamed, and succeeded in kicking his foot loose.

The wood elves pulled us higher into the air, higher still, and my ears were filled with the sound of flapping wings. The ghouls beneath us grunted and snorted, looking up at us, their fat arms reaching and clawing at the air. They weren't happy at all.

But *I* certainly was! My happiness grew as I rose higher and higher above the rioting ghouls below. Soon, the tinny sound of flapping wings drowned out the huffing protests of the ghouls.

"Don't worry," one of the wood elves said as we drifted higher. "We've got you."

But where are we headed? I wondered. *Where are we going?*

The answer was even more incredible than I could have possibly imagined . . . .

24

I'd always wanted to know where Lina lived—and now I knew.

As we rose higher, the limbs around us spread out. I could see tiny homes built on the limbs all around us! They looked like little dollhouses. The houses were made of branches and dried leaves, and they blended right in! In fact, from the ground it would be impossible to see them at all!

And there were many more wood elves, sitting and standing on the branches, their wings splayed out behind them. A few flitted in the air, very quick and nimble in their movements. I was so amazed I quickly forgot about the ghouls gathered at the base of the tree far below.

The wood elves carried me to a large branch and gently set me down. They placed Darius right next to me. I was a little frightened, being so high in the air, but I knew the wood elves wouldn't let me fall.

Lina flew in front of me and lit on my leg.

"Lina!" I exclaimed. "I wish you were bigger so I could hug you!"

"You were very lucky," Lina replied. "We almost didn't get to you in time."

I looked around. "So, this is where you live?" I asked.

"Yes, this is our home," Lina said. "You're safe—for the time being."

Below, the ghouls were quickly dispersing, one by one. They were ambling away like lost sheep. Some of them just sank back into the ground and vanished.

"We haven't seen the last of them," Deepo said, instantly appearing in the air in front of me. He landed on Darius's leg, and Darius made a motion like he was going to swat him like a bug. He caught himself, and stopped.

"It won't be long now," Deepo continued. "If they're not stopped, they'll begin taking over humans. Then, they'll take over the city."

"Take over the city?!?!" Darius exclaimed. "They can't do that! The police won't let them!"

Lina shook her head. "The police can't see them. In fact, as far as we know, you are the only two people in the city who *can* see them, and see us. You are also the only two people who have the power to help us stop them."

Have you ever showed up to class and realized you left your important homework assignment in your bedroom? That's how I felt . . . only this was ten time *worse.*

"I'm not picking a fight with any of those things," Darius said, shaking his head.

"You don't have to," Deepo told him. "But, no matter what, *they* will pick a fight with *you*. By then, it will be too late. The ghouls will take over Grand Rapids, and everyone in the city will become slaves to them—including you."

"Right now, there is still a chance to stop them," Mirak said.

"But we're just two kids," I said, perplexed. "What can we do?"

Lina flitted into the air. "I'm going to do something, Ashlynn," she said. "Don't be afraid."

It was then I noticed she was carrying a small bag, no bigger than a large marble. She opened it by pulling on a drawstring. Then, she reached one hand into the bag and pulled out a handful of what appeared to be gold dust.

She held it in front of her tiny face.

"Remember," she said to me, "don't be afraid."

Then, she took a breath and blew the dust into my face . . . and a very weird day got a *lot* weirder.

25

At first, the dust blinded me. It tickled my nostrils, and I almost sneezed.

And I was afraid. I couldn't see a single thing, but I knew I was still high in the air.

What if I fall? I thought. I felt strangely off balance, like I wasn't sure what way was up or down.

"You're all right," Lina was saying gently. "Don't worry. You're all right. Just wait a moment, and you'll be able to see."

I wanted to believe her, but I felt really odd. My body felt strange, and my skin tingled. My arms felt very heavy, and so did my legs. I felt a little groggy, too.

"I feel like I'm going to fall," I said, trying to regain composure.

"That's all right," Lina said. "We won't let you fall. Just let the magic take hold."

Magic? I thought. *What magic? What is she talking about?*

"My tongue feels really big and swollen," I said, and my voice slurred a little.

I heard Darius gasp. "Oh my gosh!" he exclaimed. "It's impossible!"

"What?" I asked. "What's impossible?" I still couldn't see a single thing, but I felt very different. I felt . . . *bigger*. Like I'd grown into an adult in only a matter of moments.

Then, I started to see a hazy gray light. I could make out fuzzy shapes.

"Better?" Lina asked, and now I could see her seated on my enormous leg.

Enormous leg?!?!

"Ashlynn!" Darius said. "You've changed! She turned you into . . . into . . . ."

He couldn't finish his sentence, but he didn't need to. I looked at my arm, which was now big, fat, and ugly. My hands were gigantic, the size of basketballs. Even my clothing had changed. I was now wearing ratty clothing, old and torn . . . nothing like the jeans and T-shirt I had been wearing!

Oh no! I thought, almost screaming. *I haven't been turned into an adult! I've been turned into a ghoul . . . which was just as bad!*

26

"What's wrong?!?!" I exclaimed frantically. "How come I'm a ghoul?!?!"

"Don't worry," Lina urged. "You're not a ghoul. It's only a disguise. It will wear off."

I was completely freaked out! I looked absolutely hideous! If Mom and Dad saw me right now, they'd pass out, just like Darius had done in the bushes! And if they knew I was their *daughter* . . . well, that would push them over the edge.

"But . . . but why?" I stammered. "Why change me into a ghoul?"

"It's the perfect way to stop the ghouls," Lina explained. "You see, as a ghoul, you'll be able to walk among the other ghouls. You will be able to go where they live, and they'll think you're one of them. Many years ago, when we first learned of the ghouls, we found humans like you—humans that could see us. We did the very same thing. We used our magic to turn one of them into a ghoul. He was able to go where the ghouls live, and stop them from taking over the city."

"But I don't want to get *near* them!" I exclaimed.

Deepo spoke. "They won't harm you," he said. "Remember: you look like one of them, now. They'll have no reason to harm you. And you will be able to get to the source of their power."

"And what's that?" I asked, already sure I didn't want the answer.

"The ghouls all eat the same kind of food, from a large trough," Lina said. "They eat a mixture of tree bark, leaves, and ordinary dirt from the ground."

"No way!" Darius said. "That's disgusting!"

"They're ghouls," Mirak said. "Everything about them is disgusting."

"But, if they eat dirt and roots, what does that do?" I asked.

"The ghouls have created a special potion made from the roots of certain trees. It's very powerful. They've been mixing their food with this potion, and that is what's giving them more and more power," Lina said. "In fact, that's what they're using to give themselves the power to take over ordinary humans."

"Like Mr. Hoffman!" I exclaimed suddenly. "We saw him today! For a moment, he was a ghoul! Then, he changed back into himself!"

"Yes, but it wasn't his fault," Lina replied. "It was a ghoul, and the ghoul was trying to take over his human form . . . but he wasn't powerful enough. But soon, the ghouls will have the power to take over ordinary humans. They'll have super-human strength. If that happens, nothing will stop them."

"But what does this have to do with me being a ghoul?" I asked.

"We've created a powder that will poison their food," Lina said. "It's the same thing we did years ago, when we had to stop them. The poison won't harm them, but it will take away their power. They'll no longer be able to surface, and no longer be able to complete their plan to take over Grand Rapids. Your job will be to go down into the ground, find their food trough, and put the powder in."

"But if you did it to the ghouls years ago," Darius said, "how come you have to do it again?"

"The poison won't last forever," Lina replied. "I wish it would. We'll have the same problem again in the future . . . but not for a long time. That is, of course, if you are successful, Ashlynn."

It sounded scary, being among all those ugly ghouls, but it didn't seem all that difficult . . .

especially if I looked like a ghoul and they left me alone.

"But there is one catch," Deepo said. "Your magic won't last for very long.

"Can't you just give me some more of that stuff?" I asked.

Deepo shook his head. "The magic doesn't work that way. Even if we had a lot more of it, you still will change back into your human form when it begins to wear off. If that happens when you're in the ground, in their home, there is no way you'll escape."

Uh-oh!

As Darius and I were lowered back to the ground by dozens of wood elves, I couldn't help but wonder if this plan was going to work. After all, it seemed beyond farfetched: it seemed totally crazy.

And I'm not the least bit ashamed to say that I was more than just a little scared! While we had been sitting on the branch high in the tree, I'd asked Lina why *I* had to do this, and why one of the wood elves couldn't change into a ghoul.

"We could," she explained, "and the magic would make us look just like a ghoul. But we would still be very small, perhaps twice our own size. The magic won't make us as big as we need to be. You, on the other hand, are three times your own size . . . the exact size of a ghoul."

I guess it made sense. Mirak went on to say that there are limits to what the magical gold dust can do. He also gave me a special bracelet with a compartment that looped around my wrist. He explained that inside the compartment was a small amount of gold dust to carry with me, and, if I needed, I could use it to 'freeze' a ghoul. All I would need to do was open the compartment and blow the dust onto the ghoul. I hoped I didn't have to use it, but it was comforting to have it.

"Why didn't you use that stuff on the ghouls when they were below us?" Darius asked.

"We would have only wasted it," Lina replied. "Besides . . . once we brought you up here, into the tree, you were out of danger."

"But what am I going to do?" Darius asked.

Lina said she'd explain more when we reached the ground.

"Great," Darius said. "I'm going to be eaten by ghouls. At least I won't have to worry about my homework assignments."

Lina gave me a small pouch attached to a long, thin, leather strap. She and Mirak tied it around my neck, and the pouch dangled like a charm.

"That is all you will need when you find the feed trough," Lina said. "Just open the bag, and dump the powder in. There will be no need to stir it, as the powder will quickly work its way through all of the food."

When we reached the ground, Lina explained where we needed to go.

"While the ghouls can come up from the ground anywhere," she said, "because you are still very much a human, it isn't possible for you to do the same. You need to find the secret doorway at Centerpointe Mall. There, a stairway will lead you down beneath the city."

I looked at Darius, and he looked at me. His mouth was hanging open. Centerpointe Mall is only a few blocks from where we live.

"Centerpointe Mall?!?!" we said in unison. "But there will be people all around!"

"Yes, and that is why your friend will be with you. He will hold your hand as you walk. If anyone asks, or if they get frightened, he can simply explain that it's one of the new costumes from the costume shop in the mall."

Well, that makes sense, I thought. *Darius will be along to help keep people from freaking out. After all, people won't be able to see the real ghouls . . . but they'll be able to see me.*

"Where is the secret door?" I asked. I'd never heard of such a thing. Then again, I'd never asked about it.

"Actually, it's a door you've probably seen every time you've been in the mall," Lina replied. "It is red with a silver doorknob."

"I've seen that," I said. "It's right near the middle of the mall. I always wondered what was behind it, because I never saw anyone going in or out of it."

Lina nodded. "Yes, that's right," she replied. "But what you don't know is that no one else can see the door except you and your friend."

"You . . . you mean no one else can see the door?"

Lina shook her head. "Only those who can see us and the ghouls. The door is invisible to all others."

"But how did a door get in the mall?" I asked. "I mean . . . humans built the mall. How did the door get there?"

"The mall was built over the ghoul's entrance," Lina answered. "It was the ghouls who created the door and the long stairway that descends to their caves. Some ghouls do not have the power to rise though the ground, and that is how they come to the city."

I guess that made sense. Or, about as much sense as anything else today. Right now, I was busy trying to figure all this out.

"But what if a *real* ghoul sees me while I'm walking with Ashlynn?" Darius asked. "Then what do I do?"

"We'll just have to hope that doesn't happen," Lina said.

"Great," Darius said, rolling his eyes. "At least Centerpointe Mall isn't far away."

"How long do I have before I turn back into myself?" I asked.

"You have about an hour in human time," Lina replied. "You should have plenty of time, if all goes as planned."

Well, as you can imagine, things were *not* going to go as planned.

Not even close.

28

"If this takes us more than an hour, I'm in big trouble," I said as we headed toward the mall. We were walking on the sidewalk, and I still felt really weird in my ghoul body. And other people thought I was weird, too! People that drove by just stared at me. I waved to them, and so did Darius. But it was just like Lina had said: people thought I was just some strange person in a costume!

"Yeah," Darius said, "if you're still down there with the ghouls, beneath the mall, and you turn back into yourself . . . that's going to be big trouble."

"Not only that," I said, "I haven't even been home yet. If I'm not home in an hour for dinner, Mom and Dad are going to be worried. Then, I'll be in even *bigger* trouble."

"What's worse?" Darius asked. "Being eaten by a ghoul, or having your mom and dad mad at you for being late for dinner?"

Darius had a point. I really couldn't worry about Mom and Dad being mad when I was going to face dozens of creepy ghouls that live beneath the city. I might be late for dinner . . . but I certainly didn't want to *be* dinner!

When we reached the mall, sure enough, some people freaked out. Mostly little kids, though, and Darius was quick to tell everyone it was only a costume. Some people actually thought I was cool looking, and came over for a closer look. One lady touched my hand and exclaimed, "Eeeww! It even *feels* real!"

More people stared as we walked through the mall, but no one ever *really* freaked out. Some people jumped and did a double-take, but when they saw Darius walking at my side, they knew I must be just wearing a costume.

If they only knew the truth!

We turned to head toward the middle of the mall, where the halls intersect. Unfortunately, I didn't see a little kid walking toward me. He didn't see me, either. Before I knew it, he had bumped into my leg. When he looked up, he screamed, horrified, and took off running. His mother had to go running after him. I felt kind of bad, since I didn't want to scare anyone . . . especially a little boy, who would probably have nightmares for a long time.

I saw the door up ahead, just like I'd seen it dozens of times before. It was strange to think no one else could see the door but Darius and me.

I tried to prepare myself mentally for what I was about to do. Was I scared?

Of course.

Terrified, in fact.

But I had to go through with it. I really didn't have any other choice . . . and the clock was ticking. I'd have to hurry.

We stopped in front of the door.

"Here we are," Darius said. "Are you ready?"

"No," I replied. "But I guess it doesn't matter if I'm ready or not. I've got to go through with it."

I checked to make sure I still had the locket dangling from the lace around my neck and the bracelet with the small container of magic gold dust. Everything was all set.

This will be over before I know it, I assured myself. *Everything is going to be fine.*

But now, we had another problem. Just as I was about to open the door, I heard a frantic scurrying of feet. Darius and I turned to see two uniformed security guards running toward us!

29

The clacking of footsteps became louder, echoing off the walls, floor and ceiling. I knew we were in trouble, but for what? Was I in trouble for scaring that poor little kid?

Probably. After all, he had been pretty scared.

My mind raced as I tried to come up with an explanation. What would I tell them? Would they take me to their security office? Would they want to call my parents? I usually don't get into a lot of trouble, but I knew my mom and dad would be pretty mad if security called them and said I was scaring people at the mall!

"Now we're in for it!" Darius whispered. "We're going to go to jail for years and years!"

"Don't be silly," I said. "They're not going to put two kids in jail."

"Yeah, but you're not a kid," Darius replied. "You're a ghoul. There's probably a law about ghouls being in the mall."

Which was also quite silly. Still, as the security guards approached, I wondered what was going to happen to us . . . and the ghouls. After all: if Darius and I were taken away by mall security, that would mean I wouldn't be able to travel into ghoulland . . . or whatever it was called.

But, as it turned out, the security guards weren't after us. They ran right by us, and their footsteps faded. They must have been looking for someone else. Oh, they both looked twice at me as they ran past, probably wondering what I was, but I'm sure they thought the same thing everyone else did: I was wearing a costume. "Let's hurry up and get this over with," Darius said.

"Easy for you to say," I said. "I'm the one who's got to go down there and find that ghoul food trough."

"Well, just be quick about it," he said, "or else you'll be down there when you turn back into your normal self."

"Wish me luck," I said, and I grasped the knob, turned it, and opened the door.

Was I scared? You bet. You would be, too, if you were in my shoes. Sure, the plan sounded simple: find the place where the ghouls eat, pour the powder in, and leave. It *sounded* simple . . . but things were about to get really complicated.

Beyond the door, a staircase plummeted down into darkness. There was no light at all, except for the first few feet. I would be descending into a wall of pitch black nothing.

"Wow," Darius said. "Maybe you should have brought a flashlight."

"Now's a fine time to think of that," I replied.

"I can leave the door open, since no one else can see it," Darius said. "That will give you a little light, at least."

I started down the steps.

"Good luck," Darius said.

"I'll need it," I replied, without looking back.

Down I went, one step at a time. Soon, I could no longer see anything at all. I found my way by feeling for the walls with my hands. And I went slowly, so I wouldn't trip over my big feet.

And the staircase seemed to go on forever. I stopped and turned around a couple of times, hoping I could see Darius at the top of the stairs . . . but he had vanished. I couldn't see a single thing.

I kept going.

And going.

Down, down, farther and farther. Lina hadn't told me how far down it went, and I began to think the stairway went all the way to the center of the earth—until I smacked into a wall. It surprised me so much I almost fell backward.

There must be some mistake, I thought. *Lina didn't say anything about a wall. How could the staircase end at a solid wall?*

The answer, of course, was that it couldn't. After feeling around with my hands for a few seconds, I found a large doorknob. It turned easily, and I pushed the door open . . . completely unprepared for what I was about to find on the other side.

31

The door opened into an enormous cave. Strange lights glowed along the walls and from above, embedded in the dirt. At first, I thought they were candles, because they weren't very bright. Then, I realized they weren't candles at all, but some sort of weird tubes of energy or electricity. I'd never seen anything like them before.

And there were ghouls everywhere, all around. Some were only a few feet away from me. They all pretty much looked the same, and they all bobbled around like they were unsure of their footing, like they were just learning to walk. They seemed to be half alive, just ambling about aimlessly.

And when I appeared in the doorway, they all stopped and looked at me.

They know, I thought, panicking. *They know I'm not one of them. They know, they know, they know!*

I was just about ready to turn around when they began shuffling around again. Most of them took their eyes off me. Whatever had happened, they must have figured I was no threat. They figured I was one of them (or so they thought!) and paid me no more mind. They wandered about, jostling each other without any clear direction, like they were half asleep.

But I wasn't fooled. I knew they were dangerous creatures.

However, *they* were fooled, and that's all that mattered. Although I was shaking from fright, the ghouls left me alone. It was the perfect disguise.

It's working! I thought excitedly. *They think I'm one of them, just like we planned. Now all I've got to do is find that trough. Find out where they eat, dump in that powder, and get out!*

But where do I begin? Lina herself said she had no clue where to find the trough. She only told me it would be big, and there would probably be a lot of ghouls around. It sounded simple, but something told me it wasn't going to be that way at all.

Being underground, beneath the mall, gave me a really strange—and scary—feeling. The ground beneath my feet was hard-packed dirt, as were the walls and ceiling. The cavern looked primitive, like it might have been dug out by hand.

I began walking—er, stumbling, that is, just like the other ghouls—and I made my way past several of them. The light here wasn't very good, and I saw some of the energy balls (or whatever they were) were different levels of brightness. Some gave off only a tiny bit of light.

And there were ghouls everywhere! There were dozens and dozens of them—maybe more. And they didn't appear to be doing anything except wandering around. None of them seemed like they had anything to do.

All of a sudden, I was knocked sideways, off balance. I nearly lost my footing and fell. A ghoul had bumped into me!

He grunted and looked at me as if to say it was my fault. I was afraid he was going to do something, but, after a moment, he moved on.

I continued on my way, wandering among the ghouls. Thankfully, it didn't take me long to find what I was looking for: a gathering of ghouls, seated around a large table. Except that it wasn't really a table. It was like a big, square tub of some sort. There were crude chairs all around it, and a ghoul sat in nearly every one. They were pawing at the contents of the tub and putting it into their mouths. They weren't even using any silverware!

Yes! I thought. *That's it! That's what I'm looking for!*

This was going to be a piece of cake. I stumble-acted my way over to the food trough, and reached up with one big, fat hand to remove the tiny bag of powder around my neck—and that's when I was struck with a freight train of horror.

The bag of powder that had been around my neck was gone!

Panic rocked through my body, and I pawed at my neck with oversized hands.

No! I thought. *I just had it! Where could it have gone?!?!*

I thought frantically, furiously. *Where could I have lost it?*

Then I remembered bumping into that ghoul.

The bag must have broken when the ghoul hit me, I thought, already backtracking my steps. I waded through the crowd of ghouls. They still gave me the creeps, especially since I was so close to them. It was a good thing they didn't know I was actually a human!

I found the place where I thought the ghoul had bumped into me. There were still a lot of ghouls all around, though, and I didn't want to do anything that would raise their suspicion. So, I just looked down at the ground while I walked about, searching for the small bag.

There! I thought, as I spotted the small bag on the ground. I picked it up. It had been stepped on, but it hadn't broken open. What a relief! Now I could finish what I came here to do.

I walked back to the ghoul feed trough, where many creatures were busy shoving food into their mouths.

Sheesh, I thought. *These guys eat like pigs. Mom and Dad would never let me eat like that at the table . . . and I wouldn't want to, anyway.*

Carefully opening the small, leather bag, I walked up to the trough. The food the ghouls were eating was gross, all right. I looked like dirt with a bunch of chopped up leaves and pieces of tree bark . . . but it had an orange tinge to it, making it look unnatural. It looked like chunky mud mixed with orange sherbet. Strange.

No matter. I had a job to do, and I was going to do it. I was going to do it, and get out as fast as I could.

I opened the small pouch. I had a little bit of difficulty, because my hands and fingers were so big. I wasn't used to them, and I struggled with the bag.

Finally, I got it open, and I looked around to make sure there were no ghouls watching me.

Nope. The ones seated around the table were too intent on eating.

I reached out casually, and emptied the contents of the pouch. I didn't see how such a small amount was going to do anything, especially without mixing it up. But Lina said all I needed to do was pour it in . . . so that's what I did.

A strange thing happened. The powder that I poured in vanished in the food, like it was sucked into the dirt. Then, I noticed that a peculiar sparkle suddenly shot through all the food. It wasn't bright, just little glints of shine here and there, spreading out through the entire trough. Some of the ghouls even noticed it, but they didn't pay much attention. They just kept eating.

There, I thought. *I hope that works.*

If the tainted food had an effect on the ghouls, I didn't see it. The ghouls didn't do anything strange or act differently.

No matter. I did what I came here to do, and it was time to leave.

I turned and made my way toward the door that would take me to the stairs and out of this creepy place. No ghouls paid any attention to me, and I felt smug, knowing I'd fooled all of them. I'd actually become one of them, and they didn't know it! Now, they would eat the food that would soon take all their power away.

I heard a commotion ahead. There was suddenly a lot of grunting and odd noises. Ghoul talk, I suppose.

I kept walking, and soon realized the commotion was coming from the doorway that led back to the stairway I had descended . . . and when I saw what was causing the fuss, I stopped in my tracks, stunned.

While I had been able to fool the ghouls, Darius couldn't . . . and two ghouls were holding him captive!

33

Darius looked absolutely horrified. On either side of him stood a ghoul, each one with a firm grasp on Darius's arms. They must have captured him in the mall and brought him down the stairs!

"Let me go!" Darius shrieked. "Let me go right now!"

The ghouls, of course, weren't about to let him go. They acted as if they hadn't even heard him.

Things weren't going to be as easy as I thought.

On my wrist, I still had the bracelet containing the gold dust Mirak had given me. Looks like I'd be using it, after all, and I sure was glad I had it.

Darius looked right at me, but he didn't recognize me. How could he? I looked just like all the other ghouls.

I started walking toward him. Other ghouls had gathered around, and they were looking at Darius like someone looks at some exotic animal at the zoo. Darius looked frightened, and his eyes darted from one ghoul to another.

"Please let me go," Darius pleaded. "Let's just forget the whole thing, okay? I'll head back up the stairs and I won't bother you at all. I promise."

The ghouls, of course, continued to ignore him.

But what were they going to do with him? I wondered. *Now that he was captured, where was he going to be taken?* I wished I'd asked Lina a lot more questions.

Thankfully, I was able to blend right in with all the other ghouls. I drew close to Darius, just like a few other ghouls, and did the same thing they were doing.

I was right in front of Darius. I tried to catch his eye, to let him know it was me, but it was no use. He was too scared, glancing around, trying to figure out what to do. I couldn't blame him. I was scared, too.

Behind him, the door stood wide open . . . and I had a plan. I would use the magical gold dust on the two ghouls that were holding Darius. That would freeze them. Then, I could grab Darius, pull him away from the two ghouls, and leap through the door.

I knew it was going to be a long shot . . . and I was right.

34

Like the small leather pouch, I had a little trouble opening the compartment on the bracelet . . . but I managed. The lid finally popped open, and I was relieved to see the small heap of gold dust. I'd had a horrible thought as I opened it, wondering if, somehow, it had leaked out. It was a relief to see the pile of dust in the compartment.

I raised the compartment to my face, held it just beneath my lips, and took a step toward one of the ghouls that was holding Darius's arm.

I hope this works, I thought as I took a deep, ghoul breath.

I brought my wrist closer to my lips, leaned toward the ghoul . . . and huffed.

A tiny cloud of gold dust misted over the back of the ghoul's head. Without waiting for a reaction, I leaned toward the other ghoul and did the same thing. Again, a small cloud of gold dust misted the ghoul's head.

Had it worked? I had no idea. But there was no more magic gold dust left, and I had to assume it had done its work.

I grabbed Darius's arm and pulled him back, away from the two ghouls. He was surprised, and I was relieved to see his two captors were standing motionless.

It worked! They were frozen!

"Darius!" I said. "It's me! Let's get out of here!"

The other ghouls standing around looked curious and confused . . . but I knew they'd figure out what was going on soon enough. We needed to get out—*fast.*

I was still holding Darius's arm, and I pulled him to the door and into the stairway. I closed the door behind me, and we started up the steps, fumbling our way in the darkness.

"They caught me in the mall!" Darius gasped as we hurried up the steps.

"Tell me later!" I said, "After we get out of here!"

I tripped on a few steps, but I managed to catch myself before I fell. It didn't take us long before we could see faint light above; the secret door in Centerpointe Mall was still open.

Seeing this, I felt a surge of energy, and I moved even faster. Darius was behind me as we took the stairs two at a time. Suddenly, we were met with white light, and the recognizable sights and smells of the mall. There was a kid nearby, and he saw us appear out of nowhere. His eyes popped, and he turned and ran. That must have freaked him out! To him, it probably looked like we came right through the wall! Thankfully, no one else saw us. It would have looked very strange to suddenly appear out of thin air!

"Let's get out of here!" I said to Darius. "Those things are going to start coming after us!"

We whisked through the mall. People still gave me weird looks. Many of them smiled, thinking I was someone in a costume. I waved to a few of them, and they waved back.

We hurried through the mall as quickly as we could, knowing the ghouls would certainly but coming after us.

But it wasn't the ghouls we had to worry about.

As we hustled by a small kiosk, I heard a lady shout:

"You! In the costume! Hold it! I want to talk to you!"

I spun to see a lady rushing toward me with a child in tow. It was the same kid I'd accidentally bumped into earlier, the one who had been totally freaked and ran away.

The lady rushed up to me and grabbed my arm.

"You should be ashamed of yourself!" she scolded. "That costume is frightening! You shouldn't be out, wandering the mall, scaring children!"

I tried to pull away from her grasp, but she held on tight.

"I'm not through with you, buster!" she said. "You scared my son, Marcus, here, half to death. How do you feel about that?"

"Gosh, lady, I'm really sorry," I said.

"We're really, really sorry," Darius echoed. "That's why we're leaving the mall, right now. We never intended to scare anyone."

And that's when I saw the movement out of the corner of my eye. Darius saw it, too.

Coming right toward us, not far away at all.

Ghouls.

They were coming for us . . . but the lady wouldn't let go of my arm!

35

"Lady, please," I begged, struggling to pull my arm from her grasp. "We really have to go."

"Shame, shame, shame," the woman said, looking at me.

Out of the corner of my eye, I could see the ghouls coming closer and closer.

The lady continued scolding me. "You should be—"

She stopped. A very puzzled expression came over her face. She looked at me closely, very curious.

Then her expression turned to horror.

"That's . . . that's not . . . not a c . . . costume," she stammered, gasping. "You . . . you're . . . *real!*"

Then she fainted!

Darius and I quickly grabbed her before she fell. We sat her down on a nearby bench, and her head flopped to the side. Her eyes were closed, and she looked like she'd dozed off. She'd had a bad scare . . . but she wasn't hurt.

"Don't worry," Darius said to her son, who was looking at his mother. "She just fell asleep. She'll wake up soon."

The boy seemed relieved, and crawled onto the bench next to his mother, who was out cold.

But the ghouls were still coming.

"Let's get out of here!" I shouted, and we took off again, weaving through the mall, trying not to make too much of a scene. I think I frightened a few people, but most seemed amused by the

strange creature hustling through the mall. Of course, they couldn't see the other ghouls, so they probably didn't worry much.

And I was glad the ghouls couldn't move as fast as we could! Soon, we'd made it to the front doors. By that time, we'd lost sight of the creatures. Oh, I was sure they were still after us, but we weren't in any immediate danger. Now all we had to do was keep away from them and wait for the magical gold dust to wear off, so I would turn back into my normal self.

"That place down there was too freaky!" Darius said as we walked. "Did you find the food trough?"

"Yeah," I said. "I did exactly what the wood elves told me to do. I sure hope it works."

We stopped at a corner and waited to cross the street. Cars went by, and lots of people stared. A few people honked, and I could see them laughing. Everyone—most people, that is—seemed to think I was wearing a costume . . . and that was fine with me.

After traffic cleared, we crossed the street and made our way back to the block where we live. We were on the sidewalk, headed home, when I recognized my dad's car. Without thinking, I waved at him. He waved back, but he gave me a really odd look.

"Oh, I forgot!" I said with a laugh. "Dad doesn't recognize me!"

We kept walking, rounded the corner to our street . . . and that's where we were met with an army of ghouls.

36

Darius and I stopped walking. Time seemed to stand still. There was no breeze, and the sky above was dappled with enormous cauliflower clouds.

The ghouls were waiting for us, it seemed. They weren't coming toward us, but, rather, just seemed to teem in a large group, each creature teetering, shuffling on ready feet. I couldn't count how many there were, but they filled the street, and spilled out over the sidewalks and into yards and driveways.

Waiting for us.

"I don't think that stuff you put in the food trough worked," Darius said quietly.

"Well, I'm sure not all of them have had a chance to eat it yet," I said. "It wasn't that long ago that I dumped it in there."

"So . . . now what do we do?" Darius wondered aloud. His voice trembled unevenly.

"Well, we know we're faster than they are," I said, "so we can outrun them. But if one of them catches us, we're in trouble."

A few ghouls turned their heads up to the sky, like they were looking at an airplane. I looked up, but I didn't see anything.

Then, a few of the creatures began swatting at the air, like they were waving away bees or bugs. Soon, all the ghouls were doing it. It was actually sort of funny . . . in a ghoulish kind of way.

"What are they doing?" I wondered aloud.

Soon, a few ghouls stopped moving, as if they were frozen.

"Hah! I know what's going on!" I suddenly exclaimed. "The wood elves are pouring that powder on them! It's freezing the ghouls! We're just too far away to see the elves, that's all!"

In no time at all, every single ghoul stood motionless. Some of them were frozen with their mouths open . . . others had their arms raised as they tried to swipe at the elves, but they were moving even slower, as if they were falling asleep.

"Come on!" I said to Darius, and we took off down the street, heading right toward the army of frozen ghouls.

Sure enough, as we got closer, I looked up to see dozens of wood elves in the sky, swarming like a buzzing, leafy-green cloud.

And did the ghouls ever look funny! They all had surprised expressions on their faces, like they were all wondering what was going on! None of them flinched, however, for which I was glad. They just remained stony and silent, like wax figures or cement statues.

Lina saw us and she swooped down, arcing and sweeping around, hovering in front of us, hummingbird-like. Deepo followed.

"Did you find the food trough?" Lina asked anxiously.

"Yes," I replied. "I did exactly what you asked."

"That's wonderful!" Lina exclaimed. "It is now only a matter of time. Each ghoul that eats will soon lose its power to rise to the surface. We will no longer have to worry about them taking over humans."

"How long will it take?" Darius asked.

"It may take a few days," Lina said. "But, one by one, their powers will fade away."

"But when am I going to change back?" I asked, suddenly very self-conscious of the fact that I was standing in the middle of the street on my own block, in plain view, for all to see. While no one could see the ghouls or the wood elves, they could certainly see Darius and me. I began imagining people in their homes thinking: *that's*

Darius Perry, out there . . . but who's the big fella in the creature-costume?

"It shouldn't be long now," Lina said, "or, I can use the magical gold dust to change you back."

I liked that idea the best.

"Let's do *that,*" I said, "only, let's go into the forest at the end of the block. That way no one will see me change back."

"That's a good idea," Deepo said as he hovered in the air. "These ghouls will emerge from their frozen state very soon. You shouldn't be around them when they do."

And so, we trundled down the block, ambling along the sidewalk. Although all the ghouls were still paralyzed by the magic dust, we made a wide circle around them. I'd had enough of them already, and I didn't want to get any closer than I had to. Above us, wood elves buzzed past, on their way to their home high in the tree in the woods. Lina went ahead of us to retrieve some of the magical gold dust.

"Boy, I'll be glad when this is all over with," I said to Darius.

"Me, too," Darius replied. "I've had enough of those gruesome ghouls."

We walked a little way into the forest. Lina found us, and she fluttered in front of my face. "This will only take an instant," she said, pouring a small amount of the dust into her hand. She blew it into my face, and I winced. It didn't hurt or anything, but the puff of air and dust caused me to squint.

Instantly, my body began changing. Within just a few seconds, I was my same old self again: Ashlynn Meyer. I looked at my arms and felt my fingers. I quickly decided that I liked *my* body much better than the ghoul's body!

"So, what now?" I asked Lina.

She flew to a nearby branch and perched, folding her wings behind her. "It will take a couple of days for all the ghouls to be affected by the food," she warned. "So, in the meantime, you'll still need to be careful."

"We will," Darius said. "If I see any of those things again, I'm not going near them."

"That would be wise," Lina advised. "Just keep your eyes open."

"I've got to pick up my backpack from those bushes and get home," I said. "I'm sure dinner is about ready."

"And I've got to see if my homework and books are still in the grass by the tree," Darius said. "I hope nobody horked it."

"Maybe a dog ate it," I said with a laugh.

"Or flying monkeys stole it!" Darius exclaimed.

We said good-bye to Lina, grateful that our mission had been accomplished. Now, no matter what happened, things would finally get back to normal. Grand Rapids was no longer in danger of being taken over by ghouls, and the wood elves could continue to live high in their tree in the forest, where they wouldn't be bothered.

But, after dinner, I realized all was still not well . . . and it began with a frantic phone call from Darius.

#

I hadn't expected to talk to Darius again that night. He went with me to retrieve my backpack, and I went with him to locate his homework. It was right near the tree where he'd left it. We said our good-byes, and I told him I'd see him in the morning.

At dinner, my dad said something funny. "You know," he said, "I was coming home and I saw your friend, Darius, up the block. He was with someone wearing a gigantic creature costume.

Whoever it was, they waved at me like they knew me."

"Really?" I said.

"Yeah. The costume looked scary. Had me fooled, for a minute."

I had to fight to keep from laughing. Of course, he would have never believed me if I told him it was me!

The phone rang right after we cleaned up the dinner dishes. It was Darius, and he sounded panicky.

"Ashlynn!" he exclaimed in a hushed whisper. *"Can you come over here?!?! Right now?"*

"Well, I was planning on doing my homework," I replied.

"It's really important!" Darius pleaded. *"I can't talk to you about it over the phone!"*

Darius sounded frightened, and I wondered what the problem could be.

"Yeah, I guess I could come over," I replied. "But I can't stay long."

"Hurry!" he said.

"I will," I replied, and hung up.

Wow, I wondered as I slipped on my spring coat and found my tennis shoes. *I wonder what he's so freaked out about? Are there ghouls around his house?*

I'd have to be careful.

"Mom, I'm going to Darius's house for a few minutes," I said.

"Don't be long," Mom replied from the kitchen.

I opened the front door and started down the street. The evening was cool, but it wouldn't be long before summer was here. I couldn't wait. Summer is my favorite time of the year.

As I got closer to Darius's house, I saw exactly what he was talking about.

There were police cars and television news crews on the street in front of his home!

38

I had no idea exactly what was going on, but I had a sneaking suspicion it had something to do with the ghouls.

Had someone been hurt? I wondered. Darius sounded all right on the phone . . . just worried. *But had something happened to someone else? Was everyone okay?*

But the ghouls weren't able to harm anyone, Lina had told me. Not unless they had been able to take over the body of a human.

And we stopped them from being able to do that, I thought. *Hadn't we?*

Hadn't we?

My heart beat faster, and I quickened my stride. Ahead, I could see a guy with a large, black television camera perched on his shoulder. He was pointing it at a man in a suit holding a microphone. He was speaking to the camera, but I was too far away to hear him.

Nearby, two uniformed police officers were talking to a woman clothed in a long, light blue robe. She was wearing a hair net and pink slippers. She looked a little silly, wearing those things outside! She was talking quickly and making a lot of wild gestures with her arms.

There were a few other people around, too, talking among themselves.

But what had happened? I wondered again. *What's going on?*

"Ashlynn!" I heard someone hiss, but I couldn't tell who said it, or where they were. I stopped walking and listened.

"Psssst! Ashlynn! Over here!"

Then, I saw Darius. He was in his backyard, frantically waving his arms to get my attention.

I waved to him and cut across the lawn, rounded the corner of the house, and met him in the backyard.

"What happened?" I asked.

"That lady saw you and called the police!" Darius explained. "She said she saw a giant creature dragging a kid down the street. She thinks I've been kidnapped by the ghoul!"

I laughed, but quickly realized the situation was serious.

"Well," I said, "you've got to go out there and tell them that you're okay, and let them know that nothing is wrong."

"But they'll ask about the ghoul," Darius said. "I can't tell them that you're the ghoul!"

"Sure you can!" I said. "And I'll go with you. After all, I *was* the one who was with you, wasn't I?"

Darius nodded. "Yeah, but—"

"But it's the *truth,* Darius. I *was* with you. We'll tell them the truth, and they'll think that the woman was just imagining things."

"Won't we get into trouble?" Darius asked.

"How?" I replied. "Darius . . . it's the *truth.* I *was* with you. And besides . . . we can't let them think that someone is missing."

Darius thought about this. "Yeah," he finally said. "I guess you're right. Let's go tell them."

But I have to admit . . . I was a little nervous. Were we doing the right thing?

We'd know in less than half a minute . . . .

39

As we rounded the front of the house, the woman in the robe spotted Darius right away. Her arm snapped out, pointing. *"There he is!"* she cackled. *"That's him! That's him! That's the boy the creature kidnapped!"*

Everyone looked at us. The man holding the television camera pointed it in our direction. I felt really nervous, with everyone staring at us.

"What's going on?" Darius asked casually, but I could tell that he, too, was a little jittery.

"I saw you with that . . . that *thing!*" the woman stated. "Just over an hour ago!"

"What thing?" Darius asked.

"I don't know," the woman replied. "A creature! A horrible, ugly creature!"

Darius looked puzzled. "I was just walking with my friend, Ashlynn," he said, hiking his thumb at me.

"Yeah," I said. "It was just me!"

"Impossible," the lady said. "The creature was twice your size! It . . . it looked like a ghoul!"

"Okay, I admit it," I said, rolling my eyes. "The wood elves turned me into a ghoul. Then, they changed me back into a girl."

Darius looked at me with wide eyes. He couldn't believe what I was saying!

However, it worked. The crowd began to break up, and people started leaving. I could hear some of them snickering and laughing beneath their breath. They thought I was making up a story, and that the woman was imagining things.

"I've got to get started on my homework," I told Darius. "I'll see you tomorrow. And don't forget what Lina said: watch out for ghouls. It might take a day or two for all of them to eat the food in the trough."

I went to bed that night, hoping I wouldn't see any ghouls. In the morning, on my way to the bus stop, I looked for ghouls . . . but I didn't see any.

A couple of days later, Lina came to my window after school.

"It worked, Ashlynn!" she said. "The ghouls are powerless!"

What a relief! Now I didn't have to worry anymore. I was safe, Darius was safe, and Grand Rapids was safe. The wood elves were safe, too, and, to this day, Lina is one of my very best friends.

But there were other things that began to bother me.

I started hearing about more strange things that were happening around Michigan. I heard about a girl and her brother who had a really terrifying experience with clowns at a carnival in Kalamazoo. Then, there was a big news story about dinosaurs destroying Detroit. That was freaky! And I also heard about a kid who had to fight off aliens in the city of Alpena, and a couple of girls my age who had battled gargoyles in the northern city of Gaylord.

All of these, of course, were stories, and I didn't know if they were true or not . . . except the dinosaurs in Detroit. I knew that was real because I saw it on the news. That was freaky!

Later in the year, on Thanksgiving day, we traveled to Bay City to visit some relatives. I have a few cousins, but Jamie Butcher and his sister, Tori, are my favorites. They're really funny. I told them all about the wood elves and the ghouls, because I knew they would believe me.

"We've heard all about weird things going on around Michigan," Jamie told me. "Why, in Saginaw, they had this big deal about giant spiders not long ago. A lot of people were freaked out. In fact, we had something happen to us."

Jamie looked at Tori, as if he was asking permission. Clearly, they were more than a little uncomfortable.

"We don't talk about it much," Tori said, "because what happened to us was so *scary*."

"What happened?" I asked.

"Well," Jamie began, "we thought they were just stories . . . at first. Until we found out that the stories are true."

"What stories?" I asked.

"About the bionic bats in Bay City," Jamie replied.

"What do you mean by 'bionic'?" I asked. I'd heard of the word, but I wasn't sure of its proper meaning.

"It means that they have super-human strength," Tori replied.

My jaw fell. "Really?!?!" I exclaimed. "Tell me what happened!"

"Are you going to freak out, like everyone else we've told?" Tori asked.

"I battled gigantic ghouls in Grand Rapids," I replied smartly. "I think I can handle a story about bionic bats."

"Okay," Jamie said, "I'll start."

Unfortunately, I was wrong . . . because what Jamie told me didn't just freak me out . . . it still gives me nightmares to this very day . . . .

NEXT IN THE
MICHIGAN CHILLERS SERIES:

#14: BIONIC BATS
OF
BAY CITY

CONTINUE ON TO READ A FEW
CHILLING CHAPTERS!

1

I can remember every single detail about what happened in Bay City that terrible summer. Every thought that flashes through my mind seems like yesterday, and every time I'm reminded of those awful events, a shiver shoots down my spine like a lightning bolt. Sometimes, I even break out in a sweat. I wonder if it will always be that way. I wonder if, years from now, I will still look back on last summer . . . only to cringe with fright.

My sister, Tori, feels the same way. She's eleven—one year younger than I am—and she, too, remembers everything that happened.

But, we don't talk about it.

Not anymore.

In fact, Tori refuses to even go out at night anymore, because she's so afraid of what might happen. She's even more freaked out about it than I am.

A few things you should know:

I don't get scared easily. Oh, I used to, when I was little. I used to read scary books before I went to bed, and when I turned off the light, I would imagine a monster beneath my bed, or a creature in my closet. Sometimes, I freaked myself out so badly that I had to sleep with the light on.

But I realized after I'd grown older that there are no such things as monsters in closets or under beds. And, after a while, I was no longer afraid. Oh, there are still things that frighten me. For instance, I don't like going down into our basement, because it seems really dark, even with the light on. I imagine there are creatures hiding behind the furnace, or tucked around some of the big storage boxes there.

There was one time, however, that I had good reason to be scared. In fact, what happened in the basement one afternoon should have been a warning of things that were to come.

Mom had asked me to go down into the basement, bring up the vacuum, and clean the living room. I wasn't all that happy about it, because I'd planned to meet my friend, Meredith Gaylor, at the school playground. She's been my friend since we were little, and my mom and dad are good friends with her mom and dad. Meredith told me that she'd caught a box turtle by the river, and she'd promised to show it to me.

"Great," I mumbled to myself as I reluctantly opened the basement door.

And that's when I heard a noise.

It was faint—not very loud at all—and it was coming from somewhere in the dark basement.

I should have turned around right there. I should have told my mom about the noise, and then maybe she would have looked into it.

But remember: I don't get scared that easily. After all, I *am* twelve years old. A noise in the basement wasn't about to scare me off. Sure, I was a little leery about going into the basement because it was so dark. But, whatever the noise was, I knew that it couldn't be anything that would harm me.

Or could it?

No, I told myself as I took a step down the stairs. *I'm not going to be afraid of anything in the basement. Not today.*

As it turned out, though, I was about to be proven wrong . . . .

2

I took another step.

Then, I reached out with my left hand and flicked the light switch on the wall. A single bulb at the bottom of the staircase blinked on . . . but there was an immediate *pop!* and the light went out.

"Great," I murmured again.

I turned around.

"Mom!" I shouted, "the light bulb in the basement just burned out!"

"Well, fix it!" came my sister's voice from the living room.

"I can't reach it!" I hollered back.

"Just leave it," I heard my mom call out from the kitchen. "Use the flashlight on the shelf. It's right by the door."

Of course. I knew the flashlight was there, because I used it once in a while. Once in a while, when mom and dad let us play outside after dark, we'd use the flashlight to play games.

I grabbed the flashlight . . . and that's when I heard the strange squealing noise again, coming from the basement. I stopped for a moment, straining to hear anything more, but the only sounds I heard were from my mom in the kitchen, and the television in the living room.

I clicked the light on and aimed it down the steps. Here, it wasn't very dark, but once I reached the basement, I knew I'd need the flashlight to find the vacuum cleaner. Without any lights, our basement is completely dark.

I descended the steps, and the wood boards creaked beneath my feet. When I reached the last step I stopped. I swept the beam around the room.

Shadows moved as the light fell over boxes, an old pool table, a chair with a sheet over it, and a treadmill that had a filmy layer of dust on it. Dad bought the contraption a few years ago, saying that he was going to use it every day. And he did, too—for about a week. Then, he moved it from the living room to the basement, where it still stands to this day. Dad says he's going to pull it out and use it soon, but he's been saying that for months. Mom wants to sell it. Me? I'd like to take it apart. It would be cool to find out how it works.

Sweeping the beam around, I finally found the vacuum cleaner. It was right where it always was: next to my dad's set of golf clubs. They had nearly as much dust on them as the treadmill.

I made my way confidently across the dark basement, following the glowing white beam. I was trying to look on the bright side: it wouldn't take me too long to clean the living room. I would still have time to meet Meredith at the playground and see the box turtle she'd caught.

I was only a few feet from the vacuum cleaner when I heard the squealing again.

This time it was louder, and I knew that I was much closer to it. I could also tell that the sound hadn't come from the floor, but from above, up near the ceiling, from a darkened corner of the basement.

I stopped moving and slowly swung the flashlight beam toward the sound. A bright white circle illuminated a shelf that was packed with all kinds of things: coffee cans filled with nails, old books, tools, and my old snowmobile boots that I'd outgrown.

But as I directed the light farther and farther up, I saw something else:

A pair of tiny red eyes, glowing back at me!

It took a moment to realize what I was seeing. The two red dots reflected the glare of the flashlight, and I suddenly realized that a pair of eyes were staring back at me.

Slowly, I raised the flashlight beam higher and higher. My heart was racing, and my mind was whirling.

And then, a shadow came into view. The silhouette of a head and ears darkened the wall. The creature squealed again, and I breathed a sigh of relief.

A mouse, I thought. *I can't believe I was startled by a little mouse.*

The tiny creature spun quickly, and vanished in with a squeal and a flurry of scratching claws. Then, I laughed out loud. It was sort of funny, now that I thought about it.

I picked up the vacuum cleaner, turned, and carried it back to the stairs. Somewhere behind me, the mouse squeaked again, and I shook my head. Mice, like monsters in the closet or under the bed, are nothing to be afraid of.

With the flashlight in one hand and the vacuum in the other, I ascended the stairs. Once again, I could hear Mom fussing in the kitchen, preparing dinner. The television was still on, and I heard Tori laugh at something. She wasn't going to be very happy to see me with the vacuum, because that meant she wouldn't be able to hear the television.

When I reached the last step I clicked off the flashlight and put it back on the shelf. Then I stepped into the hall and closed the basement door behind me. I set the vacuum down on the carpeted floor.

"I found a mouse in the basement, Mom," I called out.

"Another one?" Mom replied. "I thought your father had taken care of those things."

"After I finish with the living room, can I go to the school playground?" I asked as I unwound the vacuum cord and plugged it into the wall.

"Not for long," Mom answered. "Dinner will be ready soon."

Hot dog! I thought. After all, I was really looking forward to seeing the box turtle Meredith had caught. I'd never seen one before, except in pictures.

I switched on the vacuum and it whirred to life. Just as I expected, Tori got up from where she was sitting and went into her bedroom. Her cat, Merlin, was probably outside. Merlin is all black with white paws. Tori begged Mom and Dad for a cat until she finally got Merlin as a kitten. If that cat is anywhere close when the vacuum starts, he freaks out. He hates the vacuum cleaner.

I got to work. It wouldn't take me more than a few minutes to vacuum the entire living room and pick it up. The sooner I finished, the sooner I could leave . . . unless, of course, Mom wanted me to do something else. She'll do that, once in a while. Just when I think I've finished something and can go do what I want, she'll ask me to do something else. It drives me crazy, sometimes.

Sometimes, it's just not fair.

I rushed through the living room with the vacuum, determined to finish as quickly as I could. Actually, it didn't take me long at all. Tori left a pile of her homework on the couch, and after I'd finished vacuuming, I picked it up and carried it to her bedroom door. Then I knocked twice.

"Your homework is by the door," I said smartly, placing the pile on the floor. "I puked on it."

There was no answer from behind the door, and I grinned. We always tease each other like that. We're not mean to each other, except for once in a while. But we're always kidding around and joking with each other.

I went back to the living room. "All finished, Mom," I said, and I closed my eyes and crossed my fingers, hoping she wouldn't ask me to do anything else.

Mom came into the living room. Her hands were covered with flour, and she was wearing the apron that Tori and I got her for Mother's Day. It's white with red letters that read: KISS THE COOK. She really likes it, and she wears it all the time. What's really funny, though, is that Dad wears it, too. Dad loves to cook, and when he does, he always puts on Mom's apron.

Yeah, I know what you're thinking, and you're right: I have goofy parents. But for the most part, they're okay.

Mom looked around the living room, inspecting my work. "It looks good," she said, to my great relief.

"I'm going to go to the playground for a while," I said.

"Don't be gone long," Mom said, "and be sure to put the vacuum away before you go." Then she turned and walked back into the kitchen.

Cool, I thought. I was glad I didn't get roped into doing something else . . . like cleaning my room or washing windows.

I grabbed the vacuum cleaner, pushed it down the hall, and stopped at the basement door. Then, I unplugged the electrical cord and wrapped it around the unit. Then I picked it up by the handle.

I opened the basement door, plucked the flashlight from the shelf, flicked it on, and started down the stairs.

Fearless.

After all: there was no reason to be afraid of anything in the basement. I had a flashlight, so I could see fine. And I certainly wasn't afraid of a puny little mouse.

Still, I had a strange feeling as I walked down the steps with the flashlight in one hand and the vacuum cleaner in the other. I felt like—

Like I wasn't alone.

No. That's just silly.

Like someone was watching me.

Nope. There was nothing in the basement except a bunch of clutter—I was certain.

But I was wrong.

Something else was down there, waiting in the shadows, watching warily as I descended farther and farther into the basement, deeper into the darkness.

I should have listened to that little voice in my head that told me something wasn't right . . . but I didn't. I just kept going down the steps.

Soon, however, I would realize:

There was something down there.

Something was waiting . . . waiting for me in the darkness—and that something was only a few feet away . . . .

ABOUT THE AUTHOR

Johnathan Rand is the author of more than 50 books, with well over 2 million copies in print. Series include **AMERICAN CHILLERS, MICHIGAN CHILLERS, FREDDIE FERNORTNER, FEARLESS FIRST GRADER**, and **THE ADVENTURE CLUB.** He's also co-authored a novel for teens (with Christopher Knight) entitled **PANDEMIA**. When not traveling, Rand lives in northern Michigan with his wife and two dogs. He is also the only author in the world to have a store that sells only his works: **CHILLERMANIA!** is located in Indian River, Michigan. Johnathan Rand is not always at the store, but he has been known to drop by frequently. Find out more at:

www.americanchillers.com

JOIN THE FREE AMERICAN CHILLERS FAN CLUB!

It's easy to join . . . and best of all, it's FREE!
Find out more today by visiting:

WWW.AMERICANCHILLERS.COM

And don't forget to browse the on-line superstore, where you can order books, hats, shirts, and lots more cool stuff!

Johnathan Rand travels internationally for school visits and book signings! For booking information, call:

1 (231) 238-0338!

www.americanchillers.com

Also by Johnathan Rand:

GHOST IN THE GRAVEYARD